"I'll show you why I want to know you."

Briana pulled away, but he was too fast. He drew her to him and his mouth found hers, kissing her hungrily. Then, drawing away slightly, he looked into her eyes.

"For the past four months," Brand said slowly, "all I did was look at you. I watched you work, move your body, saw that shuttered look in those green eyes of yours. And I wanted to know what hid behind that look. I wanted to touch you and hold you and make love to you."

His hands caressed her, and suddenly she began to tremble. She pushed at his hands. "I don't want to make love," she said and her voice shook.

It was a lie; she wanted him to go on. "I don't want to make love," she repeated. But her voice lacked conviction....

KAREN VAN DER ZEE is an author on the move. Her husband's work as an agricultural advisor to developing countries has taken them to many exotic locations. The couple said their marriage vows in Kenya, celebrated the birth of their first daughter in Ghana and their second in the United States, where they make their permanent home. The whole family spent two fascinating years in Indonesia. Karen has had several short stories published in her native Holland, and her modern romance novels with their strong characters and colorful backgrounds are enjoyed around the world.

Books by Karen van der Zee

These books may be available at your local bookseller.

Don't miss any of our special offers. Write to us at the following address for information on our newest releases.

Harlequin Reader Service
901 Fuhrmann Blvd., P.O. Box 1397, Buffalo, NY 14240
Canadian address: P.O. Box 603,
Fort Erie, Ont. L2A 5X3

KAREN
VAN DER ZEE

time for another dream

Harlequin Books

TORONTO • NEW YORK • LONDON
AMSTERDAM • PARIS • SYDNEY • HAMBURG
STOCKHOLM • ATHENS • TOKYO • MILAN

For my parents-in-law and my brother John,
three very special people.

Harlequin Presents first edition January 1987
ISBN 0-373-10950-4

Original hardcover edition published in 1986
by Mills & Boon Limited

CHAPTER ONE

THE big man leaned casually back in his desk chair and shook his head. 'I doubt you'll want the job,' he said carefully, his grey eyes raking over her in slow, deliberate appraisal. 'It doesn't pay much.'

Briana felt a flare of irritation, more with herself than with him. She'd dressed inappropriately, she realised. Her stylish, expensive clothes belied the fact that she was in need of a job, or at least this job.

'I don't need much,' she said quietly, looking right at him, feeling a flutter of uncertainty at the sight of the aggressive chin and the cool grey eyes. He wasn't a handsome man—his face too irregular and rugged for that—but he was big and masculine. The arms in the short-sleeved shirt were strong and tanned and covered with dark hair. Under the heavy eyebrows the grey eyes looked light in the dark face. His hair was thick and unruly and she liked the reddish-brown colour.

'Have you ever done this kind of work before?' he asked politely. 'Do you have any experience in rehabilitation?'

She shook her head. 'No.'

'Any particular qualifications?'

She hesitated, seeing in her mind Tommy's round little face. It wouldn't add up in his eyes, most likely. *I had a little brother . . .*

'No,' she answered.

The heavy eyebrows lifted and his eyes mocked her. 'Not even a degree in social work?'

'No.' And not one in psychology, psychiatry, brain dysfunction or neurology, either, she felt tempted to add, but was quiet. She couldn't let this man goad her.

7

Her degree was in fashion design, not worth mentioning in this context. It would probably generate a burst of sarcastic laughter.

'I'm sorry, Miss Calloway, but the requirements are very specific for this job. I'm looking for a person . . .'

Briana knew exactly what kind of person Brand Edwards was looking for. Julie, the present supervisor, was leaving her job after ten years. And what he wanted was another Julie. Briana had known Julie for a number of years and she was well aware of the responsibilities of the job. It was Julie herself who had suggested Briana apply. She'd supplied her with the written job description to read and had explained the more specific details of the duties and requirements. Briana straightened in her chair, pushing a heavy fall of dark, curly hair behind her ear.

'I can do it. I can learn.' She tried to make her voice calm and decisive.

'What makes you think you can do this sort of work?' he asked impatiently.

Briana took a deep breath. 'Instinct.' She looked straight into his frowning face. 'A sixth sense, whatever it's called. And determination.'

He was not impressed. 'What makes you think,' he repeated, 'that you can handle these people?'

For a moment she wasn't sure she'd heard right. Then she realised he was testing her.

'I wouldn't,' she said coolly.

'Oh?'

'I wouldn't *handle* them, Mr Edwards. I would *work* with them.'

He surveyed her in silence, speculation in the grey eyes. 'Working in a sheltered workshop isn't everybody's idea of a glamorous job,' he stated at last.

Briana gritted her teeth. 'I'm not looking for glamour,' she countered. She'd seen enough glamour in her life. She hadn't come to Leesburg, Virginia for glamour. 'I'm well aware that most people are not inspired by the prospect of working with physically and mentally handicapped people, Mr Edwards. It makes them uncomfortable even to look at someone in a wheelchair, or talk to a person who can't speak as we do. Well, I'm not uncomfortable, Mr Edwards. I know what to do when someone has a seizure, too. That's what happens now and then, isn't it? And I can handle the paperwork. No problem.'

He raised his eyebrows in mild surprise. 'Can you use a sewing machine?'

'Yes. And I can type too,' she said caustically, finally losing her cool. 'And cook dinner from scratch.' What did he think she was? A nitwit?

He ignored her remarks. 'How old are you?'

'Old enough. And I shouldn't have to remind you that it's against the law to ask me my age.'

'Not a day over twenty,' he stated calmly, a flicker of humour in his eyes now.

'I'll consider it a compliment,' she said sweetly. She was twenty-five and looked it, and he wasn't going to trick her.

'Ah, too smart by far,' he said, pretending regret.

Briana looked down at her hands. Beautiful hands, beautifully manicured, long nails polished a dark coral. A gold ring with a brown topaz encircled her right ring finger. Wrong, all wrong, she thought. Why hadn't she thought about it? These hands did not belong in a place like this. Her Paris suit did not belong. She looked up, determined to give it one more shot.

'Mr Edwards, I happen to know that you haven't had much luck finding someone for this position. I know that Julie is leaving at the end of the month. Someone has to take over from her, or you'll have fourteen men and women who can't work because there's no one to organise the jobs. You have a large contract with a delivery promised two weeks after Julie leaves. It's one of your biggest customers, the

dental supply house. You can't afford to lose them.'
She saw anger flare in his eyes. He straightened his
chair, leaning forward, arms on the desk.

'I don't need you to point out my problems, Miss
Calloway,' he said coldly. 'But I must admit, you're
very well informed. By Julie, I presume?'

'She's *worried*!' Involuntarily Briana leaned forward
in her chair as well. 'She feels a great sense of
responsibility for her workers and she's worried about
what'll happen if you can't find anyone to take over
from her. She can't possibly stay. You know that.'

His chair squeaked over the linoleum as he pushed
it back. He stood up, his eyes hard and cold, his
massive frame frightening by its sheer size. 'Miss
Calloway, please leave your name and phone number
with the secretary on your way out. Don't call us,
we'll . . .'

'. . . call you,' she finished for him. She came to her
feet and swung her bag over her shoulder, glaring hard
at the angry face before turning to leave the room.

She'd blown it royally. Briana sighed in resignation as
she drove the little silver-grey Volvo out of the
workshop parking lot. Stacks of timber lay in the back
of the building waiting to be transformed into pallets
and crates and wooden boxes. Eighteen men of various
capabilities spent their days sawing lengths of wood
and nailing them into containers for the transport of
fruit and nuts and many other products. In the other
room, on the far side of the building, fourteen men
and women made fabric sample books for upholstery
companies, assembled small parts for computers and
dental equipment, sorted, collated, and stuffed
discount coupons into envelopes for home delivery.
This was the place where Julie worked, organising the
jobs and assigning the work to the different
handicapped workshop employees.

Julie and Brand Edwards had worked together for

the past ten years. She'd come to help him shortly after he'd started the workshop in an old bar. After several years he had managed, with the considerable help of the community, to get a new building. Now Julie was leaving because her husband was being transferred out of state, an opportunity he could not pass up.

Briana swung the Volvo on to the sun-baked road and stepped on the accelerator. Phew, the car was like an oven. She switched on the air-conditioner and shifted uneasily in the hot seat. July in Virginia was almost as bad as in Florida.

Julie had sung Brand's praises for the past ten years. Because of his dedication and sheer stubborn persistence there was now a place for handicapped people, who would otherwise spend their days in idleness and boredom, to do useful work. Work that gave them self-respect, more independence, and money to spend. Work that other people or businesses didn't want to take on.

Briana sighed and pushed a stray curl of hair back from her forehead. She felt deflated, somehow. Until a month ago she hadn't even known the job was available, hadn't even entertained the idea of doing anything in this direction. Fashion design did not exactly prepare one for work with handicapped people.

But she needed something to fill the emptiness in her life, and fashion design wasn't going to do that. She needed a burning passion, something to forget herself in, to spend her energies on something, or someone, besides herself. She was tired of the life she'd been leading, a hollow existence full of hollow people. When was the last time she'd been happy in the last two years? Really happy? Not once, not one day since that fateful afternoon when all her illusions had shattered in a single second.

There was a lot of happiness in that workshop— happiness and joy despite all the tragedy. She'd seen it when she'd visited Julie there, watched the people struggling with their bodies and their minds, trying so hard to do their best. They were happy to be at work, happy to be with friends who did not treat them with pity or revulsion or fear. Nobody minded that they talked funny or sat in a wheel chair or rocked their heads or dragged their feet. She remembered entering the work room—the curious eyes on her, the faces breaking into smiles, the friendly greetings. They were all so eager for acceptance, for respect, for friendship.

'Oh, forget it,' she said out loud to herself, swerving the car to avoid a rock on the road. 'You're not going to get that job, and who can blame the man? You've never held a real job in your life. You've accomplished nothing useful. So forget it. Sell Grandma's house and go home to Florida where you belong.'

She didn't want to go back to Florida, to the sterile black and white apartment that had been her home for the past three years, and that she'd never liked anyway. She didn't want to sell Grandma's house. As a child she'd spent so many happy summers here. She could see the house now, peeking out from behind large pine trees. It was only a small place, a brown wooden house with a brick chimney and a covered front porch. In back was a big garden and a shed, and an old chickenhouse, now empty, and a row of berry bushes. Picking berries had been what she'd loved most as a child—picking them and eating them at the same time with the juice running down her chin and staining her shirt.

Briana parked the car next to the house and walked up the porch steps, almost tripping on a loose board when her high heel got caught under it. Her eye caught her reflection in the living-room window, slim and elegant in her light summer suit with the silk blouse underneath it. Perfect attire for going to job interviews according to books and magazines, but she had the uneasy feeling that jeans and a cotton blouse might have been a better choice this time. Brand Edwards had not been impressed by her appearance, had probably dismissed her as a serious candidate because of it.

The telephone rang as she opened the front door and she rushed to the kitchen to pick up the receiver.

'Hi, Briana? It's Julie. I'm on my lunch break and I hoped to catch you at home.'

'I just got in.'

'What did Brand say?'

'Don't call us, we'll call you.'

Julie groaned. 'What happened?'

'Very little. He seemed unimpressed from the moment I walked into the door. He . . .'

Julie laughed. 'Briana, I've never seen any man unimpressed by you. All that gorgeous hair and those green eyes knock 'em flat every time.'

'Don't exaggerate, Julie. Brand Edwards probably doesn't like green eyes. Anyway, he asked me my qualifications, which, of course, I don't have. That didn't help. I don't even have a resumé, you know. I've never actually held a real job, Julie. Designing clothes for a boutique hardly counts.'

'You ran your friend's dress shop for five months.'

'That's not exactly relevant experience. Anyway, he wanted to know what made me think I could do this work, and then he told me that it wasn't very glamorous and didn't make much money, et cetera, et cetera. And . . . oh, well, I don't think I did a very convincing job on him.'

'I'll go have a talk with him. He's so damned pigheaded about this. What he wants is perfection, and he doesn't realise that he's simply not going to find it. I mean, he wants a relevant college degree, several years of experience in rehabilitation and so on, and then he's offering a lousy little salary and no opportunities for promotion, because there's no place to go after this job. This is the top of the line, and the bottom as well, come to think of it, and . . .'

'*You've* done this job for ten years.'

'That's different. I grew up with it. I mean, we started so small in the beginning. And Briana, there's no reason why you can't do it. You're a very sensitive person and I liked the way you handled yourself when you visited my room. The people liked you. They talked about you for the rest of the day.' Julie laughed. 'They wondered if you were a movie star. Anyway, I'll have another talk with Mr Perfect. I'd better head back to the cafeteria before all the food is gone. See you!'

Briana replaced the receiver. She picked up the shoes she'd kicked off and went into the bedroom to change into shorts and T-shirt. This was the room she'd always slept in when she stayed at Grandma's. It had been her mother's bedroom once. Pink flowered wallpaper, faded now. A double bed with a patchwork quilt that showed signs of wear and tear. There was a white painted dresser and some shelves on the wall that still held her mother's childhood books, dolls and other toys.

Like the bedroom, the rest of the house had never changed. Still the same wallpaper, the same worn linoleum, a collection of china cats, lacy doilies on the coffee table and arm-chairs, pictures of family members. As a child she'd found comfort in the sameness of the place. She'd liked it the way it was, with the frilly curtains in front of the windows and the plaques on the walls.

She thought of her own spacious apartment in Florida with its black-and-white colour scheme, its glass and chrome, its designer furniture from Italy. A place too cold and stark for comfort. She didn't care if she never saw it again.

After she had changed her clothes she wandered through the house, wondering what to do about all the old books, the stacks of women's magazines that Grandma had saved for years and years, the countless little knick-knacks, Grandma's clothes in her bedroom. There was nothing of value anywhere. Nobody would want any of these things that had meant so much to her. Briana knew she didn't have the heart to pack it all up and put it outside for the garbage collection. How could she throw out a whole lifetime of memories?

Faint resentment curled inside her. Why was her mother not here taking care of it? After all Grandma was *her* mother. Some of her own things were still here in the bedroom of her childhood. But her mother had not wanted to come and do it.

'You do what you think is best, Briana,' she'd said.

'But Mom! I don't know! Your things are still there, and the things that belonged to Grandpa and, well, you know more about it than I do.'

But her mother had shaken her head mutely and Briana's heart had gone out to her. Her face had looked drawn and white. The death of her mother had hit her hard, even though it had been expected. Even though Grandma had been old.

She studied the pictures on the bookcase. A snapshot of her mother as a young girl. Grandma and Grandpa's wedding picture. Photos of each of their parents—her great-grandparents—strange-looking people with stern expressions and drab clothes, standing stiff and straight, staring woodenly ahead. There was a picture of Tommy, too, and her heart ached as she looked at the sweet, smiling face. With a sigh, Briana turned away, found a dusting cloth and carefully dusted the picture framews, the china cats, the plaques on the wall.

'I talked to Brand,' Julie said two days later. She'd come by after work and they were sitting at the kitchen table drinking coffee. Julie was thirty-three, short and slightly chubby. Her soft brown hair was shaped in a shiny page-boy cut, which gave her an oddly old-fashioned look. 'He blew his top,' she went on. 'He said I was wasting his time, and mine, by trying to convince him to hire you for the job. If I didn't know him so well, I'd be scared to death of him. As it is I think I'm the only one in that office who isn't.' She grinned. 'Kathleen, the secretary, and Margaret, the counsellor, practically shake in their shoes at the sight of him. Anyway, I had no luck, which ruined my day as you may be able to understand.'

Briana frowned, stirring her coffee. 'What does he have against me? Except for the fact that I'm not qualified. I mean, I got some very negative vibes from him. I don't think he liked the look of me.'

Julie laughed. 'I bet he liked the look of you too much for his own comfort. I'll be frank with you.'

'Please do.'

Julie's blue eyes looked right at her. 'He said he didn't want some spoiled little rich girl doing her do-gooder work in his shop only to take off when she got bored with it all. He doesn't believe you are a responsible person. He doesn't believe you're serious.'

Briana let out an exasperated sigh. 'Wowee! What makes him think all these things? He doesn't even know me!' Anger began to seep slowly through her. 'Who does he think he is to come up with that kind of judgment?''

Julie swallowed a mouthful of coffee and shrugged. 'Oh, Brand *knows* who he is. No lack of confidence there. And when he's made up his mind it's very difficult to change it.'

'But why does he think these things? Just from looking at me?'

'I guess so, I don't know. What did you look like?'

'Like myself!'

'Which is pretty good. What did you wear?'

'A suit. A cream-coloured suit with a pale green blouse. Nothing exotic or flamboyant.'

'But superbly elegant, no doubt,' Julie said drily. 'I'm envious of your clothes, believe me, but I wonder if a little too much elegance didn't give our friend Brand the wrong impression.'

'Since when is it wrong to dress well?' Briana challenged irritably, waving her hands in agitation. 'It's ridiculous! The man is stupid and presumptuous to jump to all those conclusions about me just because . . . oh, forget it.' She dropped her hands on the table in a gesture of defeat.

'I don't want to forget it,' Julie said, shaking her head in disagreement. 'I can't afford to. There's no one else scheduled for an interview—I asked Kathleen—and I'm due to leave in less than four weeks.'

'What is he going to do when you leave?'

'I have the sneaking suspicion that he's counting on my loyalty to stay on until he does find somebody.'

'But you're moving to South Carolina!'

'I know, I know. He figures Jack can go by himself and I'll stay here with my mother for the time being. I don't know. He probably didn't think about the logistics. He's made a lot of sacrifices for this place himself. He probably thinks I owe it to the shop to do the same.'

'You've got to be kidding!'

'Oh, no I'm not. You don't know our Brand. He is totally absorbed in the workshop. There's nothing else in the world that counts quite as much.'

'So what's going to happen?' Briana couldn't help being intrigued by this man, irritating as he was.

There was a devilish gleam in Julie's eyes. 'I have a plan. He'll be gone for a couple of days next week, Tuesday and Thursday. I want you to come into work with me and I'll start familiarising you with the set-up. What do you think?'

Briana frowned. 'He may not see me there, but he'll find out of course.'

'Oh, sure! Let's just hope it won't be until Friday. We have nothing to lose, so it doesn't matter, does it?'

She frowned. 'I don't know.' It didn't sound right, sneaking around behind his back. Then she shrugged. 'Oh, all right.'

'It's for his own good,' said Julie, sounding like a mother. Then she grinned. 'Don't look so doubtful. We've got to do something, haven't we?' She stood up. 'I've got to go. I'll see you tomorrow night then. Don't forget the dessert!'

Briana laughed. Julie had invited her for a barbecue and she'd offered to bring dessert. 'How many are coming?'

'We'll be eight all together. Oh, and don't dress up. Just jeans or trousers.'

Briana felt a pin-prick of suspicion. 'Is Brand invited, by any chance?'

Julie grimaced. 'I hoped you wouldn't ask.'

'I wasn't born yesterday, Julie. You gave it away.'

'Don't go backing out now. I need your dessert!'

'Oh, I'll come, don't worry. Brand Edwards doesn't frighten me.'

'Good, he shouldn't. He's really a wonderful guy once you get to know him.'

A wonderful guy, my foot, Briana thought as she watched Julie climb into her car and drive away.

As per Julie's intructions, Briana dressed in jeans and a wide, blue-and-white striped blouse. She arrived at Julie's house finding both couples there already, but no Brand. Jack was busy lighting the barbecue and Julie was in the kitchen tossing a salad. Briana put the French berry tart she'd made for dessert on the counter and Julie goggled.

'You *made* that?'

'Anything to use up all those berries.'

'It looks gorgeous. Must have taken ages to make.'

'I ain't got nothin' but time,' she said, grinning. 'I'll go out and meet your friends.'

After a few polite niceties to the other guests, she wandered off and looked around the garden. Julie loved growing flowers and there were masses of them everywhere. She heard the sound of a car and looked up. A battered Pontiac station wagon drove up by the side of the house and stopped. A moment later Brand jumped out and slammed the door behind him. She steeled herself at the sight of him, determined not to be impressed. Yet she knew she wasn't unaffected by the sheer masculine appeal of the broad shoulders, the cool, confident look of him as he strode across the grass to where Jack was tending the barbecue.

It would be impossible to avoid him with only eight people there and it didn't take long before she found herself face to face with him. The grey eyes looked at her coolly and her heart lurched. She wished he weren't quite so big and intimidating. She took a deep mental breath.

'Hi,' she said lightly, determined to be cool.

He inclined his head slightly, the grey eyes under the heavy brows looking at her blandly. 'Hello, Miss Calloway.'

It sounded so formal, she couldn't help smiling.

He cocked one eyebrow. 'Did I say something funny?'

'No, no. You sounded very proper, very formal.'

'And that's a cause for amusement?'

'Only for a moment,' she said, straightening her face and looking at him quasi-solemnly. She gestured at the steaks sizzling on the barbecue. 'This looks delicious, don't you think, Mr Edwards?'

He gave her a long look. 'Would you care to dispense with the Mister and Miss?'

'Only if it doesn't make you uncomfortable,' she said gravely.

Something flickered in his eyes. 'It won't make me uncomfortable.'

'Oh, good. My name is Briana.'

He nodded. 'I know. I presume you known mine?'

'Brand. Means *fire* in German. Did you know that?'

'I did. Do you speak German?' His tone was carefully polite. He probably couldn't care less whether she spoke German, or Turkish, for that matter.

'Only a little. My paternal grandmother was German. She used to live with us. She was determined I learn the language and she always spoke German to me. She died when I was eight. I don't remember much.'

'It would come back easily if you tried.'

'Maybe I should go to Germany for a while.' This was the most uninspired conversation she'd had in a long time. She wondered how long they could keep it up.

'An expensive proposition.'

'True. And I don't even have a job.' She almost bit her tongue off. What a stupid thing to say! She didn't need a job to go to Germany. She could pack up tonight and go any place she pleased.

The mockery in his eyes was hard to miss. 'I don't believe you need a job at all.'

'Oh, but I do!'

'Fallen on hard times?'

'You could say that.' Maybe not financially, but certainly in other ways.

'I'm afraid the Loudoun Sheltered Workshop is not the place to start looking.'

She smiled sweetly. 'You made that abundantly clear. You have any suggestions?'

'How about modelling? Or acting?'

She frowned as if giving this serious consideration. 'Not really my thing, I'm afraid.'

'What is your thing, Briana?'

'Well, let's see. I'm a good cook. I can put on four-course dinners for twelve, or twenty at a pinch. Maybe I could work in the workshop cafeteria.'

He arched his eyebrows. 'Where did you learn to do all that cooking?'

'In my own kitchen. I'm a very talented person. Or did you imagine spoiled little rich girls never lifted a spoon in the kitchen?'

His mouth quirked. 'I can tell Julie has been talking to you.' He didn't seem embarrassed in the least.

'She has. It's amazing to find out what opinion you have of me, having seen me for ten, fifteen minutes flat. You must be a creative person with a very fertile imagination.'

He inclined his head. 'Thank you,' he said drily. His eyes focused on something beyond her. 'Jack is giving us the high sign. The steaks must be ready.'

He said very little to her for the rest of the evening. She kept herself busy helping Julie, trying not to pay attention to Brand, but her eyes kept searching him out.

When Briana handed him coffee and dessert, he glanced up and gave her a faintly sardonic smile. 'Julie told me you're the creator of this sumptuous-looking confection,' he commented, looking down on the plate she handed him. 'Is it safe to eat?'

It took her a fraction of a moment before comprehension dawned, but before she could answer he pointed at the sprig of mint.

'This isn't hemlock, by any chance?'

'Unfortunately not. I checked at the supermarket, but they were all out.'

He grinned, and it was the first time she'd seen him do that. 'In that case I will enjoy this without worry.'

She went home later that night, knowing that Brand had most likely not changed his mind about her. She didn't know where to begin to convince him she was capable of doing the job, that she wasn't a flighty-headed number who'd take off again in a few weeks. She fell alseep thinking about going to the shop behind his back, wondering what he'd say when he found out.

* * *

Tuesday was an exhausting day. There was so much to learn and her underlying sense of unease made it more tiring. Every time the door opened she looked over her shoulder, expecting Brand Edwards' massive frame to come into the workroom. It was ridiculous of course, a fear born only out of guilt. Brand was safely out of town and wouldn't be back in his office until the next day.

She began by reading the files of all the customers—the dental equipment company, the upholstery company, the computer corporation, and a number of other, smaller ones that regularly put in orders. She learned about job sheets and work sheets and client evaluations. After lunch she was too tired to read more, so she spent time observing the employees and talking to Julie about how she assigned the different jobs to the different people. Each person had his or her speciality. Some were good at sorting, but had poor finger dexterity. Some of the women were trained on the sewing machine and one man, a deaf mute, handled a cutting machine that cut lengths of fabric into smaller sampler pieces for the unholstery swatch books.

Jill, the girl on the sewing machine, was hemming bath sheets, an order put in by a health club which had furnished the large bolts of pale green terry cloth material. Jill sat in a wheelchair in front of the machine, her dark head bent shyly to her work as Julie and Briana stopped beside her. Julie lightly touched the girl's shoulder.

'You smell nice, Jill. Perfume?'

The girl looked up and nodded. 'It-it's Joy. I-I-I-I bought it yes-yesterday.'

'I like it. You did a good job on the sheets. There's only one I think we should do again. You're getting the hang of it aren't you?'

Jill smiled, happiness in her face, but she said

nothing, bending down again to her work, a long, dark braid falling over her shoulder.

'They amputated one of her legs half a year ago,' Julie told Briana later. 'Her mother said the doctors are afraid they'll have to take the other one as well.'

Briana listened silently as Julie told her Jill's medical history, which covered a variety of problems attributed to brain damage during birth.

'The girl over there is Tammy. She's Brand's sister. She's retarded. She had meningitis when she was small, went into convulsions, and was in a coma for days. She's had a lot of special schooling. Her major problem work-wise is that she has a short attention span. She gets restless and we have to find different things for her to do.'

Briana talked to the workers to get to know them, asking them about their work and what jobs they liked to do best. Some were very shy, others more talkative, eager for an audience. One mentally retarded young man, Jim, shook her hand when she arrived, asked her how she was and favoured her with great big smiles all through the day. He was big and bulky and wore striped coveralls with bulging pockets, full of what sounded like change and keys.

From Julie she heard about their backgrounds—some sad and tragic stories, some happy. She heard of loneliness and poverty and illness. Of endless doctoring and repeated operations to make limbs work and bodies function better. She went home that night exhausted both physically and mentally, marvelling at the strength some people had when there seemed to be no money, no help, no hope for them.

So, she said to herself, why do I feel sorry for myself? She opened a can of chicken noodle soup and poured the contents into a small pan, then added water and put the pan on the stove.

No, it wasn't true. She didn't feel sorry for herself. There just seemed to be a lack of happiness in her life, as if she'd used it all up in that one glorious, delirious year. But it had only been an illusion, a terrible mistake. It was over now and it was better that way.

She put the soup, some crackers and cheese on a tray and took it out to the front porch to eat. It was a balmy summer evening, the air fragrant with the smells of hay wafting in from a field nearby. The house was located on a country road not far out of town and she loved the feeling of freedom and space, the wide blue sky, the serenity of the land around her.

A young couple came strolling down the road, a small boy toddling along between them. He waved at her when he saw her on the porch and the parents smiled and called out a friendly good evening.

All the next day she thought about the shop, feeling a strength and conviction growing in her. She wanted the job. It was a chance to make herself useful, to do something that mattered. For two years now she'd been at a loose end, having no purpose in life. Now she was struggling for breath, new air, new space to start again.

It was with a renewed determination that she went back on Thursday and spent another exhausting but rewarding day at the workshop. At four-thirty the workers left in a bus that took them to their various homes, or to the group home where a number of them lived together with a supervisory staff. Briana stayed behind to help Julie finish up. They checked the completed work, organised the jobs to be done the next day and cleaned up. It was almost six by the time they were done. The door opened as Julie reached out to switch off the light in her dark little office and Brand came in.

For one moment Briana thought her heart would stop. She stared at Brand, who regarded her coolly, hands on his hips.

'Miss Calloway, I'd like to see you in my office, please.' He was calling her Miss again, and his tone promised nothing good. Her body tensed. She looked at Julie, who was glowering at Brand, her hand still on the light switch.

'You just about scared me senseless!' she accused. 'What are you doing here?'

'I'll talk to you later. Miss Calloway?' With an imperious lifting of his eyebrows he gestured at the door. She followed him to his office, her heart thumping wildly in her chest. Oh, damn, she thought, this isn't going to do me any good. He opened the door, letting her in ahead of him, then firmly closed it. He sat down in his chair behind his desk and leaned back.

'Have a seat, please.'

'I'd rather stand.'

'As you please.' He gave her a long, penetrating look. 'Please do not be deceived in thinking that I don't know what has been going on behind my back.'

Briana looked at him stonily, saying nothing. She tried to stay calm. This ape of a man wasn't going to intimidate her!

He crossed his arms in front of his chest and tipped his chair back a little further. 'What do you think you will accomplish, Miss Calloway?'

'I'm not sure. The worst that could happen is that I will know considerably more about the job of supervisor. Making a decision is always done best with the most possible information.'

He raised one eyebrow. 'A decision? What decision?'

'My decision of whether I want to work in your shop.'

Incredulity flickered briefly in his eyes, then was replaced by a look of mild mockery. 'Nice try, but no go. In case it has not penetrated the little grey cells, Miss Calloway, I'll repeat to you that I have no intention of hiring you for this job.'

'Have you found someone else?'

'It's no concern of yours whether I have or not.'

She shrugged lightly. 'I'll presume you haven't. May I ask you why you think I cannot do this job?'

'You're not qualified—neither by education nor background.'

'Background? What's wrong with my background?' She couldn't help feeling on the defensive. Her background was the American dream to the detail, at least until she'd turned twenty-one and had made the worst mistake of her life.

'You're the daughter of Geoffrey Calloway of Miami, raised in luxury and comfort. You don't know much about country living as far as I can tell. You don't know anything about the kind of people we deal with here in this county. You married, at the age of twenty-one, an infamous playboy by the name of Cliff Crossley and . . .'

Colour drained from her face. 'How do you know that?'

He shrugged. 'It wasn't hard to find out. Normally we check with former employers and references. In the absence of these, I did a general background check-up. Nothing out of the ordinary.'

She struggled with her anger. 'It's all irrelevant to whether I can do the job or not!'

'In my opinion it's very relevant, Mrs Crossley.'

'Don't call me that!'

'It's your name, isn't it?'

'No it's not! And I would appreciate it if you stopped digging around in my past. There's nothing there of any interest to you. You have no right, no right at all!'

He sat upright and the chair landed on its four legs. 'All right, I'll make you a deal. I'll stop digging in your past and you stop interfering in my job and in my shop. I don't want to see you here again, understood?'

She clenched her teeth, turned and walked out of the office without a word. She hoped fervently that

Brand Edwards would not be able to find anyone for the job. She'd like to see him crawling when he came to ask her to take over. Briana laughed to herself as she got into her car. She couldn't quite see Brand Edwards crawling, but it was an interesting idea.

She drove back through Leesburg. She liked this place, a small historical town full of colonial buildings and interesting small shops. Living here would be very different from living in Florida. It would be good to make a change, to get away from the apartment and the memories.

She dreamed of Cliff that night, happiness and anger strangely mixed up. Scenes of their honeymoon in the Caribbean Islands, sailing, swimming, snorkelling, playing tennis. Cliff laughing, saying he loved her. Scenes of their life in the apartment—friends, parties. Then a replay of that horrible afternoon when her life had collapsed around her. The pain fresh and deep, she struggled awake, sobs wrenching from her shaking body. She pressed her face into the damp pillow, trying to calm herself. She hadn't dreamed of him for months. He wasn't worthy of her dreams or her thoughts. 'Bastard,' she whispered into the pillow.

She spent the next day clearing out a closet full of old magazines, boxes of fabric scraps, an old radio, a box of spare parts of various kinds. She carried everything out to the shed, not really wanting to throw it out. Her arms and shoulders ached when she was finished and she stood still for a moment, breathing in the fragrant country air. It was lovely here—so still and quiet with only the sounds of insects and birds chirruping in the trees.

And then another sound. Steps behind her. She turned and found a tall blond man coming towards her across the lawn, carrying a brown paper grocery bag. He was the man she'd seen walking down the road with his wife and son.

'Hi,' he greeted her, smiling. He wore denim shorts and a yellow T-shirt and he had a lean, athletic build.

'Hello.' She wiped the damp curls out of her face, smiling back hesitantly. He had brown eyes, which looked interesting with the blond hair, and strong white teeth in a tanned face.

'I'm Ross Paxton. I live down the road and I'm here with the Welcome Wagon.' He grinned as he handed her the bag. 'Only joking. I thought I'd say hello and bring you an offering from the abundance of my vegetable garden.'

Briana took the bag from him. 'Thank you.' She looked inside and found several oddly shaped tomatoes, red and ripe, some lettuce and carrots and green onions. 'This is wonderful! Thank you very much.'

'I never saw a For Sale sign up,' he commented. 'I didn't realise someone had moved in.'

'The house wasn't sold. It was my grandmother's. She left it to me.'

He studied her with obvious interest. 'Are you going to live here?'

Her eyes swept the countryside. 'It's tempting. I'm considering it, but I'm not so sure about the winters. It gets cold here, doesn't it?'

He grinned. 'Depends on where you come from.'

'Florida.'

He nodded. 'It gets cold here.' He looked back at the house. 'So Mrs Andrews was your grandmother. She was a great old lady. I liked talking to her. I'd bring her vegetables once or twice a week and she'd always invite me in for coffee and cake, or whatever. People are very friendly in these parts. I like living here.'

'You haven't lived here very long?'

'I bought my place last fall, but I didn't move in until this spring. I had an apartment in Washington before.'

Briana was still holding the bag of vegetables and slowly lowered it to the ground. Everything he said was in the first person singular. 'Do your wife and son like it here too? It's quite a change from city life.'

His eyebrows shot up. 'My wife?' Then he laughed. 'Oh, Marianne! She's my sister. She was here for a week because her husband was off at some convention. They live in an apartment in Alexandria and the kid likes it here. He wants to go for walks all the time. So we walk. They went home this morning.'

She was curious to know what he did for a living, but didn't want to ask. Should she ask him in for a cold drink or a cup of coffee? The idea made her uncomfortable. No, better not. He was a stranger, after all.

'By the way,' he said, 'what's your name?'

She laughed. 'I'm sorry. I'm Briana. Briana Calloway.'

He extended a hand and his eyes smiled into hers. 'Nice to meet, you, Briana.'

His hand was big and firm and she liked the feel of it. 'Listen,' she said on impulse, 'would you like some blackberries? I have more than I know what to do with.'

'Blackberries? Great, I'd love some.'

She'd picked some earlier that day and she went into the house to get them. 'Here you go,' she said, handing over the plastic container. 'They're very sweet, don't need any sugar.'

'Thank you, I appreciate it. And now I'd better be off. Please let me know if you need help with anything. My house is the first one on the other side of the old train tracks.' His eyes were laughing into hers. 'The white one with the red door.'

'Thank you.' She watched him as he took off across the lawn with long, easy strides, then went inside and put the vegetables away.

*   *   *

After dinner, Briana sat at the kitchen table with an old shoe-box full of photographs and began sorting through them. There were baby pictures of her, school pictures, a snapshot of her in a girl-guide uniform. There were photos too of her little brother Tommy, always smiling, his eyes slightly crossed. The last one had been taken shortly before his death and she stared at it a long time. Tommy would have been eighteen now. He could have been working in a place like Brand Edwards' workshop. He would have liked that.

On the bottom was a framed photo wrapped in paper. She took off the paper absently and felt her heart lurch when she looked at her own wedding picture.

She looked beautiful in her white lace wedding gown, her eyes shining, her face radiant. Cliff looked stunning in his dark suit. Irresistibly handsome. Charming. She had been so in love with him, so hopelessly, helplessly in love. And she had been happy that first year, deliriously happy.

How could she have been so stupid, so blind?

Slowly she disassembled the silver frame, careful not to break the glass, and took the picture out, ripping it in two.

CHAPTER TWO

SOME days later Briana received an invitation to a farewell party for Julie, which was given the week before Julie was due to leave her job. Briana was pleased to have something to look forward to. The day before the party Julie called. No one had yet been found to take over for her, Julie told her, sounding concerned.

'I've told him I'm absolutely, positively leaving and he'd better not count on me after the first. I've told him I want you in the shop for this last week so there's someone who'll know something. I suggested to him to hire you on a temporary basis, so I'd like you to see if you can't make some sort of deal with him. That is if you still want the job.'

Briana laughed unbelievingly. 'You've got to be kidding! He practically threw me out last time I talked to him.'

'The situation has become considerably more desperate.'

'He can call me any time. He has my number.'

'I've got a better idea. Did you get that party invitation?'

'I did.'

'Are you coming?'

'I'd like to.'

'Good. Brand will be there too. Maybe in more convivial surroundings it'll be easier to talk to each other. Have a couple of drinks. Don't hate him too much.'

Briana laughed again. 'I don't hate him, Julie. The problem is that he is less than enamoured by me.'

'Do something about it!'

'Like what? Be charming and seduce him? I don't think it'll work with him. He's not in the least impressed by me. He's been digging in my closet and came up with a juicy titbit of information that didn't help at all.'

'He's been *what*?'

'Checking up on me. And he didn't like what he found.'

'I can't believe he did that!' Julie was aghast. 'That's not like him at all!'

'Well, he did. He said it's normal procedure to talk with former employers and check the references, and since I had none of these, he did a general sort of check-up.'

'What did he find that he didn't like, or shouldn't I ask?'

Briana shrugged. 'He didn't seem to feel that my marriage to Cliff reflected positively on my character.'

There was a silence. 'That was a rotten thing to bring up!' Then a sigh. 'Briana, you've got to believe that he's only doing this for the benefit of the shop. What I mean to say is that that's really all he cares about. Personally he wouldn't care if they'd dragged you out of the slums of Karachi or if you were a college professor. To him it's all the same, you know. But when it comes to the shop he's . . . I don't know what to call it . . .'

'A fanatic?'

'Well, sort of, I guess. Totally dedicated, really. The shop is his baby so to speak and he doesn't like to take unnecessary chances. He's given it all he's got. He's made a lot of sacrifices for this place. He's worked like a maniac for years. You have no idea what it took him to get it going.'

'Okay, okay, I get it. Stop singing his praises.'

'I just wish you wouldn't judge him too harshly.'

Briana gave a bitter laugh. 'I'd appreciate it if he didn't judge me too harshly, either.'

'Why don't you try to get to know him a little better? It'll be a nice party. See if you can't get him to take you on for a month or two, to give you a chance to prove yourself. I don't think he'll find that perfect person he's looking for in a hundred years, and in the meantime you'll be there doing a terrific job.'

'Why do you have so much confidence in me, Julie?'

'I've known you for a long time.'

'That's true, but . . .'

'No *but*! Anyway, I've got to go now. I'll see you tomorrow at the party, all right?'

'I'll be there.'

Saturday evening she stood in front of the small wardrobe, hair still dripping from her shower, and wondered what to wear. Most of her clothes were in Miami and she hadn't brought any party clothes. Anyway, if she wanted to impress Brand, wearing a chic outfit wasn't the way to do it. Her eyes rested on a simple summer dress with narrow straps and she wondered if that would do. People didn't really dress up for parties any more. Even jeans were seen at the most formal affairs.

There has to be a way to deal with a man like Brand, she thought as she pulled the dress over her head. She wondered what it might be. She wanted the job. She couldn't stay here without a thing to do. How could she possibly convince him to take her on, if only for a few months? Well, maybe she could figure it out tonight.

The party was given by the Chairman of the Board of Directors of the workshop. It was held in the garden of his home, at the edge of Leesburg. It was a magnificent old colonial house, white painted clapboard, with shuttered windows, a wrap-around porch and a sweeping lawn all around. Tall, old trees fringed the garden where long tables were set up to hold the food and drink.

A good number of people were already there when Briana arrived and she looked around for familiar faces. Julie and her husband Jack were there, and a few people she had met before, but most she'd never seen.

Having introduced herself to the host, she was directed towards the improvised bar and asked for a glass of tomato juice.

For a while she talked to Julie and Jack, keeping an eye out for Brand, who seemed to be late. Mingling at parties was nothing new to her and after an initial introduction by Julie, she had no problem keeping herself engaged in innocuous conversation. She was looking over the food at the table—canapés, a variety of cheeses, dips, fried potato skins, liver pâté— when she became suddenly aware of a presence behind her.

Turning around she found herself looking at Brand, who regarded her coolly.

'Hello, Mr Edwards,' she said in her most polite voice.

'Brand,' he said. 'Didn't we take care of that before?'

'Last time we met in your office, you reverted to Miss, so I thought I'd better not be too familiar with you. I don't want to spoil whatever chance I have to get in your good books.'

'I'd say your chances are nil, so I wouldn't worry about it.'

Briana gave him a long, assessing look. 'I wonder what you have against spoiled little rich girls,' she said casually. 'Did you have a bad experience with one?'

A dangerous glint sparked in his eyes, then was gone. He gave her a mocking smile. 'Now who has a fertile imagination?'

She smiled sunnily. 'Oh, but I'm not using my imagination, just my female intuition.' And she hadn't been far wrong, the expression in his eyes only moments earlier had told her that.

He rolled his eyes. 'God preserve me from female intuition.'

'Men, of course, are not burdened by anything as untrustworthy as intuition,' she commented with mild mockery.

'We males use our instincts,' he returned.

'Disliking me is based on instinct?'

His eyes narrowed slightly. 'Instinct of self-preservation.'

Tilting her head, she gave him an amused smile. 'I find it interesting to think you're afraid of me,' she said lightly.

'Oh, I'm not afraid of you, Briana. Just wary.'

'I wonder why.'

'It's that look about you. You're used to getting your way, aren't you? Anything you want, you get.'

She stared at him. That *look* about her? *What* look? What was he seeing in her she didn't know about? She was dismayed more than anything else. 'You're wrong, you know,' she said slowly. 'The things I wanted most, I didn't get.' She turned away abruptly, afraid she'd said more than she wanted him to know. 'Well,' she said brightly, 'I think I'll try some of this food.' Taking a small paper plate, she selected some cheese and crackers. Someone else struck up a conversation with Brand and she slipped away and joined a small group of people who stood admiring an exotic plant.

At least Brand had talked to her. It hadn't been a promising conversation, but he could have ignored her altogether.

The talk around her changed to diets. The green bean diet, the Boston diet, the buttermilk-and-bran diet, and a variety of others she'd never even heard of. A tall blonde with faded blue eyes and a pointed nose had a lot to say. She was as skinny as a popsicle stick with prominent ribs and collar-bones and had the most dreadful time keeping her weight down. 'And sometimes, you know, I get this craving, this *insane* desire for a baked potato . . .'

Briana wandered off in search of more stimulating conversation. She moved around, listening to the trials and tribulations of working in a hospital, the arrogance of doctors who didn't listen to the nurses, and other medical horrors. The men were discussing taxes, real estate, and politics.

Out of sheer boredom, she went back to the table for more food.

'I don't believe we've been introduced.'

Briana turned her head to find a dark, strikingly handsome man next to her.

'We have not.'

'My name is Christopher Marland.' He held out his hand.

She put her plate and glass down and extended her hand. 'Briana Calloway.'

'Briana. Not a very common name.' The dark eyes looked her over appreciatively.

'No.' She disengaged her hand and picked up her plate again, feeling the familiar flutter of distrust, feeling herself turn stiff and unfriendly.

'Are you a friend of Julie's?'

'Yes. And you?' she asked politely.

'I'm a member of the Board of Directors.'

'I see. Have you been since the beginning?'

He smiled. 'From the time they were in the barn dismantling old cars. Fascinating to see how it all developed.'

'Tell me about it.' She'd heard all about it from Julie. It would be interesting to hear another opinion.

He was more than willing to talk, and she stood listening, as she had most of the evening. It was, in some respects, a different story. Brand was only mentioned in the most cursory fashion. He told her about the difficulties in establishing the workshop—troubles with the local government, problems with state regulations, aggravations with red-tape clerks, lack of adequate funds. Until finally there had been money for a new building, partially from a government grant and partially raised with the support of the community. Someone had donated the land. An architect had donated his time and services for the design. Civic clubs and churches organised fund-raising affairs of all kinds.

'What I find most interesting,' he said in a rather professorial way, 'is the fact that the shop runs on doing nuisance jobs, the sort of thing that many other factories don't want to deal with. Not only are we providing work for handicapped people, we're providing a service for many industries and businesses. So the benefits go both ways.'

She nodded her appreciation. 'I heard that Brand Edwards has been the most instrumental in getting the workshop going,' she said casually. 'I was told that he worked for practically nothing in the early years.'

His eyes narrowed slightly, but his mouth was smiling. 'Certainly, he has made a great contribution ...' His eyes focused on something behind her. The smile widened insincerely. 'Here's the great man himself. Brand, have you met Briana Calloway?'

He nodded. 'I have. Hello, Briana.'

'Hello, Brand.'

'Briana is very interested in the workshop,' said Christopher. 'I've been telling her about it, but I expect you can do better.'

'You know as much as I do,' Brand stated coolly. 'There's your wife, by the way. She was looking for you.'

Irritation flitted across Christopher's face. 'Well, yes. I must be going.' He presented Briana with a most charming smile, made his excuses, and took his leave.

'Not a great friend of yours, I can tell,' Briana commented casually.

Brand shrugged, as if Christopher Marland was unworthy of discussion. 'Would you care for another drink?' he inquired politely, his eyes resting on her empty glass.

'Yes, please.'

He reached for her glass, the big hand briefly touching her fingers as she handed it to him. 'A Bloody Mary?'

'Without the vodka please.'

She watched his broad back as he retreated to the bar. He was tall with a powerful build and was undeniably masculine. He wore pale grey slacks with crisp pleats and a dark blue leisure shirt, open at the neck. She wondered what he would look like in a suit and tie. Magnificent and quite overpowering, she decided. He returned with her drink only moments later.

'Julie told me you worked for five months in a clothing store,' he said casually as he handed her the glass.

For a moment she was at a loss for words. 'It was only a small shop and it wasn't really a job.'

'Didn't you do anything?' There was mild mockery in his voice.

'Oh, sure. I ran the place. I was helping out a friend who was having a baby. I was only going to keep things going for six weeks until she could come back, but . . .' her voice trailed off. There was nothng more boring than the troubles of people you didn't even know.

'But what?'

'There were medical complications. She couldn't come back to work until five months later, so I just kept going.'

His grey eyes looked at her sharply. 'Why didn't you tell me about that?'

'It didn't seem exactly relevant to the qualifications you were looking for.'

'How many other people worked in that place?'

'Only four.'

'And how did you do?'

'I kept things rolling. No disasters.'

'What makes you think that doesn't qualify as a job?'

She shrugged. 'I was only taking over to help out a friend. And I didn't draw a salary.'

His eyebrows shot up. 'You didn't get paid?'

'No.' She sipped her tomato juice.

'Why not?'

'Because I didn't want it. The shop was relatively new and not quite established yet. My friend did offer to pay me, but I knew she couldn't really afford it. Her husband had been out of work for three months. They needed the money more than I did.'

'I hope she's a very good friend,' he said drily.

'She is. I've known her since grade school. She's been very good to me when I needed help.' She looked straight at him. 'I'm not a soft touch. I wasn't being taken advantage of, if that's what you're thinking.'

His lips curled in a faint smile. 'Okay, I believe you.'

She took another swallow and glanced around the garden. 'It was a nice idea to give Julie a party,' she commented.

'She deserves it. Ten years is a long time and she was a tremendous help when we first started in the barn.'

'Why did you do it? Start a sheltered workshop, I mean.'

He shrugged. 'There seemed to be a need for it.'

'I suppose having a sister like Tammy influenced you,' she said carefully.

'Yes.' He gave her a long, intense look. 'What influenced you to come and apply for Julie's job at the shop?'

Her hand clamped tightly around the glass. 'I've

always had an interest in what happens to handicapped people.'

'Why?'

She bit her lower lip, looking down at the glass in her hand. 'I had a little brother who was born with Down's syndrome. He died when he was twelve. He was the sweetest kid I've ever known. Everybody loved him. When he died I was ... devastated.' She swallowed, looking at him. 'Ever since then, when I see someone like him, I wonder what would have become of him, where he would have fitted in when he grew up. Society isn't always easy on people who are different. Well, I don't need to tell you.'

There was a silence. Her feet were beginning to ache. She'd been standing around for hours, it seemed. She was aware of his scrutiny, his eyes on her face. Why did she suddenly feel so depressed?

She shook her hair back, the curls swirling around her head, as if to shake free of the feeling. 'I've known about the workshop for a long time,' she said into the silence. 'I used to hear about it from Julie when I came here from Florida to be with my grandmother. I visited her workroom now and then.'

'Brand!' An elderly woman with silver-blue hair stood smiling next to them. 'I've been looking for you!' She turned to Briana. 'Sorry, honey, I didn't mean to interrupt. I was just tickled pink to see him. I've got something to tell him.'

'Never mind.' Briana smiled politely. 'I was just leaving.' She nodded at Brand and before he could say anything the silvery-haired lady started talking and Briana made her escape.

The workshop secretary called early Monday morning. 'Mr Edwards would like to see you at two this afternoon if it's convenient.'

For a moment Briana couldn't believe her ears. He was going to offer her the job, there was no doubt. A sense of wild triumph took over the surprise. Then came the nasty desire to make him suffer a little. She could say two o'clock was not convenient, but she could fit in an appointment on Wednesday afternoon. The impulse faded quickly. It was petty and unworthy and would waste valuable time.

'I'll be there,' she said.

She dressed in jeans and a red polo shirt and put on a minimum of make-up. He was sitting at his desk when she was ushered in by the secretary, a dizzy-looking blonde who seemed none the less quite efficient.

'Have a seat, please,' Brand said, putting down his pen and leaning back in his chair.

She sat down, trying hard to look relaxed and not show her inner excitement. There was certainly no agitation to be seen on Brand's face. Cool and collected as ever.

'I would like you to consider taking over Julie's work temporarily, say for three months,' he said without preliminaries. At least he didn't beat around the bush. She appreciated that. Neither did he offer any apologies. She wasn't sure if she liked that.

'Why?' she asked.

'There are no other alternatives at the moment. The other applicants are unsuitable and this is Julie's last week. I need to buy some time.'

'To look for a suitable person to take over on a permanent basis?'

'Correct.'

'I'm not considered suitable for long-term employment, but I'll do for a short time?'

'I don't even know that,' he said coolly. 'And neither do you. You haven't done this work before.'

He had her there, she had to admit. She looked straight into the cool grey eyes. 'All right, I'll accept the offer.'

'Thank you.' His face showed no reaction, no surprise or relief.

'When do you want me to start?'

His eyes ran over her and she felt a tightening in her stomach. 'How about right now? You seem to be dressed for the part.'

'Fine.' She came to her feet, but he held up a hand before she could move away.

'Wait a minute, not so fast. Don't you want to hear about the details of the agreement? Salary, health insurance, that sort of thing?'

'Oh.' She slowly sat down again, feeling slightly stupid. 'I suppose so.'

He looked at her narrowly. 'You won't be working for nothing here, although it's not a fat salary we offer.'

'I didn't come here to get a fat salary,' she said stiffly.

'It must be nice not to have to worry about money,' he commented drily.

Anger flared inside her and it took an effort to control it. 'I know you don't approve of me for some obscure reason, but we could work together better if you wouldn't make it so obvious.'

He gave her a long look. 'I apologise for that last remark. It was uncalled for.' He pulled some papers towards him. 'All right, let's get going.'

The paperwork completed, she spent the rest of the afternoon with an elated Julie. It was well after six when they were finished for the day. Brand's beat-up old Pontiac was still in the parking lot when they left the quiet building. Dark clouds had gathered at the horizon and the air felt muggy and oppressive.

'Looks like a thunderstorm brewing,' commented Julie with a frown. 'Well, take care. I'll see you in the morning.'

The house looked forlorn in the grey light. Briana parked the car and went inside. There was a feeling of emptiness in the house, as if no one lived in it. The very air seemed dead and unused.

For the first time in weeks she looked around her critically. It was still the same house, but now that her grandmother no longer lived in it, it seemed to have changed. It was different, stagnant. It was just an old house with worn furniture and faded wallpaper. Without Grandma it's nothing, she thought sadly. No warmth, no loving feeling about the place. It needs a warm, living person to make a house a home.

Later, in bed, she thought about the house, about her life, about her job at the shop. Would she be able to do the job to Brand's satisfaction? And when the three months were up, would he hire her permanently?

If she was going to stay at the shop, she'd make the house her own. Make it a home for herself.

Briana had never worked so hard in her life. Once Julie was gone the burden of the job was solely hers. Feeling the pressure of her responsibilities, she could have done without Brand's constant presence. He seemed to be making a habit of coming into her workroom at odd moments, exchange a few friendly words with the workers and then depart again. They were always happy to see him and they all liked him, which made Briana feel even more on the defensive. The moment he entered the room, she could feel herself grow tense.

It took time to really get to know the people working for her—their strengths, their weaknesses, their peculiarities. They seemed to take to her, helped her when she didn't know or remember something, laughed at her good-naturedly when she made a mistake. Only one really caused her a problem.

David was nineteen and mentally retarded. He kept walking away from his work station, talked incessantly and kept others from doing their jobs. When she wasn't looking he took away people's scissors, papers and other material, causing an uproar.

Briana waited for a week, gently admonishing him. It did not help. She set up a room divider and had him work in isolation. It did no good. He sang. The room divider fell over by accident. He lost his stapler. He produced very little and whatever he did finish was so badly done it needed doing again. Briana checked his job sheets of the previous weeks. He had done well. He was perfectly capable of doing the work he was assigned to. In desperation she called Julie who was in the middle of packing up her house.

'I'm having a disciplinary problem.'

'Tell me about it.'

'It's David.' She told Julie what was happening. 'He's acting like a little kid, testing me, seeing how far he can go.'

'And how far can he go?'

Briana was taken aback by Julie's question. Then she took a deep breath. 'Well, not much further. I've about had it with him.'

'What are your inclinations?'

'To send him home and tell him he can't come to work for a few days. It will give all of us a little peace if nothing else.'

Julie laughed. 'I knew you'd do just fine. Don't let him walk all over you. He'll shape up when he sees who's boss. That's really what he wants to know.'

Her conversation with Julie gave her a lift, a sense of confidence that her instincts were leading her in the right direction.

The next day, after another minor David-induced disaster, Briana decided that more drastic measures were called for. At the end of the day, she called him into her office, a little room off the main work floor.

'David,' she said in a businesslike tone, 'I'm not happy with your work or your behaviour. You've been bothering other people and you've been bungling your work ever since I came here. I'm afraid that until you

decide to do better we can't use you here in the shop.'
She handed him an envelope. 'This is a letter to your
mother explaining the situation. If you feel you can
work without disturbing the others and do a good job
again you may come back next Monday.'

Disbelief, then panic spread across his face. 'I
wanna work!' he shouted. 'I-I-I can't stay home all
day!'

She shook her head determinedly. She could not
give in to pleading now. 'I'm sorry, David. For the
next few days you'll just have to stay at home. You can
think about what you're going to do on Monday.'

'No!' he shouted. 'You can't make me!' He stamped
his foot and swung his arms wildly.

'David,' she said gently, 'the bus is here. You'd
better go. They're waiting for you.'

He stormed out of the office and Briana let out a
deep breath. Poor David. She felt sorry for him. Well,
maybe this would straighten him out. Slowly she came
to her feet. She felt exhausted. There were several
boxes of assembled parts for dental equipment that
needed to be checked. Briana looked down at the
boxes and sighed. She'd better take them home and
work on them tonight. She could watch TV or listen
to some music while she worked. Right now there was
some sorting to do to get ready for tomorrow and a bit
of paperwork that needed attention.

After a simple dinner she installed herself on the
living-room floor and put a tape of Gheorghe Zhamfir
on the casette player she'd brought with her from
Florida. There was nothing of interest on TV and the
news was over. Surrounded by boxes, a cup of coffee
within reach, she began work.

The delicate, airy sounds of the flute trilled through
the room, making her feel light and relaxed. Her
thoughts drifted here and there without much
direction as she worked and the hard knock on the
front door jolted her right out of her absorption. Her

legs were stiff from sitting in the same position for too long and she was amazed to find it was almost nine.

Who in the world could it be? She wasn't too happy opening the door at night. The window next to the door gave her sight of a tall male standing in the shadowed darkness and even without the detail it didn't take much to recognise Brand's bulky shape. Her heart lurched in immediate nervous reaction and her hand automatically opened the door to let him in.

CHAPTER THREE

HIS expression did not promise a neighbourly visit of the friendly variety and Briana could feel her stomach tighten in apprehension. It wasn't difficult to guess why he had come.

'Please come in,' she said, smiling bravely. He stepped inside silently and she closed the door on the warm summer night air. He wore faded jeans and a striped shirt that accentuated the broad chest and shoulders. A wide leather belt encircled his waist. She averted her eyes and waved at a chair. 'Have a seat.'

He ignored that, his grey eyes angry, his jaw rigid. 'I want to know what happened in your department this afternoon.'

The flute music quivered around them incongruously and she reached over to turn off the tape player. 'I assume you're talking about my suspension of David Wakefield?'

'Precisely.' Thumbs hooked behind his belt, feet slightly apart, he waited for her answer.

Tossing her hair back, she looked directly at him. 'Ever since I took over from Julie he has been a chronic nuisance and his work is abominable,' she said calmly. 'He was distracting everyone in the room. I tried everything I could think of and nothing worked. I had no choice.'

He scowled. 'David has never been a problem before. And he's been employed here for over a year.'

Briana gritted her teeth. Stay calm, she admonished herself. Don't let him get to you. 'Well, he has been a problem these past ten days,' she countered mildy. 'And not only for me. He has annoyed everyone in the room. It started as soon as I was in charge. As long as

47

Julie was still there he was doing just fine.' She shrugged lightly. 'He's putting on a performance just for me, to test me. I checked his work records and what he has been producing the last ten days was nothing compared to what he did earlier. He's goofing off.'

He leaned slightly forward, eyes shooting fire. 'Did it ever occur to you to talk to me about it?' His voice was low with restrained anger.

Instinctively she took a step backward, nearly tripping over one of the boxes on the floor. 'As a matter of fact it did, but I decided against it.'

'Why, may I ask?'

'I'm in charge of the department. I don't feel I should come running for help every time I have a problem. And I felt capable of handling this one. There seemed no need to bother you.'

'Well, I'm bothered! I had a furious Mrs Wakefield on the phone telling me in no uncertain terms what she thought of you. She wants her son back at work tomorrow.'

She could feel her heart begin to beat a nervous rhythm and she straightened her back in defence. 'I don't want him back tomorrow,' she said with quiet determination.

'And if I tell you to take him back?'

She anchored her feet to the floor. 'You'd be wrong.' Her voice was still under control. 'A couple of days at home will do him good. He deserves it. And everyone else in the room deserves a little peace. He's been purposely testing me and I have to show him the limits.'

He gave her a long, hard look. 'You seem to be very sure of yourself.'

'I wouldn't be doing this work if I didn't have some confidence in myself or my abilities. And if it makes you feel any better, I did call Julie to find out what she thought.'

'And what was that?'

'She didn't tell me what to do. She asked me what my inclinations were and I told her. She seemed to think I was on the right track.'

'She didn't, by any chance, tell you to see me?'

'As a matter of fact, she didn't.'

His grey eyes bored into hers. 'From now on, if there is any more trouble of this nature, I want to be informed. Is that clear? I don't want you to make a habit of dismissing people. The very reason for the existence of the workshop is so there's a place where people like David can come to work and have a useful life.' He turned on his heel, opened the door and walked out before she found any kind of words to answer him.

She sat back on the floor amid the boxes, trembling now with anger. She hated him. She hated his arrogance and his distrust. She hated the way he looked at her.

David was not at work the next morning. The others initially showed signs of relief which was soon replaced by concern. Where was David? Was he sick? Was something wrong? There was a strong bond between them, a friendship that overlooked the problems and forgave the mistakes. So Briana explained what had happened.

'I think David likes you,' Tammy said shyly.

'He *likes* me? He sure had a funny way of showing it!'

Tammy shrugged. 'I just think so.'

'I th-th-th-thhink he misses Julie,' Jill added. 'I-I-I miss Julie too.' She smiled shyly at Briana. 'But we like you too.'

The morning went by in blissful peace. Just before lunch Brand called her into the office.

'I spoke to Mrs Wakefield,' he began without preliminaries, 'and told her I stand by your decision and that David cannot come back to work until Monday.'

'Thank you.' She should be grateful for his support, but didn't feel it. It was terribly difficult to feel anything but anger and resentment. She stared at him stonily.

He looked down on a form on his desk. 'I have your phone number here. Is there any reason why I couldn't get it from the operator last night? She said you weren't listed.'

Briana shrugged. 'The phone's not in my name. I have to get it changed.'

'I see.' He frowned. 'And what were you doing last night with all those boxes spread out all over the room?'

So he had noticed. 'I was working. Checking the assembled parts for the Mansfield Company to see that they were done right.'

'At nine o'clock at night?'

'The deadline is next week.'

'So it is. Will you make it?'

'Yes.'

'I'm glad to hear it.' He looked down at his desk, dismissing her. She had the impulse to slam the door behind her, but controlled it. After all, she thought bitterly, I'm a well-brought-up little rich girl.

Late Sunday afternoon the phone rang.

'Hello Briana-with-the-green-eyes. Ross here. How about sharing a pizza with me?'

Briana was slightly taken aback by this unexpected invitation and didn't answer immediately. Ross had come by twice more with vegetables from his garden and they had chatted for a few minutes before he had left again.

'Hey, are you still there?'

'Sorry. I ... eh ...' It was the end of an interminable weekend. The aloneness was getting to her. The house felt stuffy around her. 'I'd like that.'

'Great. Come on down the road and I'll shove it in the oven.'

She'd been wide awake at six that morning, the entire day stretching out endlessly before her. She'd decided to go to church. It had felt right to do so, maybe because she'd always accompanied her grandmother when she was here to visit. After church the afternoon had sleemed endless and empty. Going to Ross for a pizza might save the day.

She changed from shorts into jeans, put on a clean shirt and combed her hair. She looked in the mirror and put on some lipstick.

The late afternoon sun filtered through the trees as she walked down the shadowed road to Ross's house. Other houses, modest old-style homes, stood just off the road, surrounded by greenery and flower beds. You're crazy, she told herself. You don't even know this man. You don't know what he does or what kind of guy he is and you're going to his house for a warmed-up frozen pizza. You may end the day raped and murdered and buried in his back garden and no one would even know where to start looking for you.

The red door stood open. She knocked and he called out from somewhere in the house, telling her to come in.

The spicy smell of pizza cooking drifted towards her. So far so good. She stood in the living room and looked around. The coffee table was stacked high with serious-looking volumes, piles of typewritten papers and a number of empty coffee cups.

Ross came in, wiping his hands on a towel, grinning. 'Sorry. I was on my knees mopping up a quart of orange juice. Don't look at the mess. I've been working all day.'

'On Sunday?'

'Oh, is it Sunday today? I lost track.' There was laughter in his eyes. He studied her for a moment, head tilted slightly to the left. 'You look like Little

Girl Lost. Come into the kitchen with me, if you don't mind.'

The kitchen was small and cosy, but obviously modernised with a dishwasher and new cabinets. The small table was laid for two with rustic ironstone plates and colourful napkins.

'Sit down,' he said, pulling out a kitchen chair. 'Say, do you always look so serious?'

'I didn't know I looked serious.'

'You do, very. How about a beer?'

She shook her head. 'No thanks. Some juice would be nice.'

'Sorry. It went all over the floor. How about some wine? Or I have Coke or iced tea.'

'Iced tea, please.'

He gave her the drink, then took the pizza from the oven. 'I fancied it up a little. Hope you don't mind. Those prefab jobs never have enough cheese on them.'

There was enough cheese on this one now, bubbling happily. 'Looks delicious,' she said, watched him as he cut the pizza into large wedges. 'Why were you working all day today?'

'I had to get a job done,' he said drily. 'As a matter of fact I worked all day yesterday too, until all hours of the night. I fell asleep with my head on my arms. Most undignified.' There was a glint of humour in his eyes. 'I'm a researcher, by the way.'

'What kind of research?'

'You don't want to know. It's boring in the extreme.'

'Try me.'

He straightened his face, looking sombre and grave. 'I'm on the research staff of a congressional committee studying the cost overruns in the Defence Department.'

'You're right. Sounds deadly ... sorry, no pun intended.'

'It is. Deadly I mean. Especially at two a.m. Here,

have a piece.' He slid a wedge of pizza on her plate, trailing melted cheese. 'And what about you?'

'What about me?'

'What do you do for a living?'

'I just started work at the Loudoun Sheltered Workshop. I'm a supervisor. It's only temporary, though.'

He took a swallow of beer and lowered the can on the table. 'I think I know the place. Just outside of town out towards Washington, right?'

'Yes.' She took another bite of the pizza. It was not bad with the extra cheese on it. She noticed he was sprinkling his liberally with hot pepper flakes. 'You like hot food?' she asked, changing the subject.

'I do. The hotter the better. And you?'

'I like Indian food. Curries, any kind.'

'Mexican is my favourite.'

After they'd finished the pizza he showed her his garden, a neatly staked out affair growing lusciously and abundantly.

'This is what I enjoy doing when I finish work,' he stated. 'Very relaxing. After dealing with military matters all day, this is a very peaceful place.'

'What else do you do besides work and garden?' There didn't seem much time left over if he worked Saturdays and Sundays.

'I play racket-ball when I'm in town. And I take willing women out to dinner.' His eyes were laughing into hers. 'Let me get you a paper bag for this stuff.'

'I think I'd better go,' she said after he'd put the various vegetables in a bag.

He sighed. 'I'm afraid so. I've got to get back to work.' He walked her to the door.

'Thanks very much for dinner and for this.' She hugged the bag to her chest.

'It was my pleasure,' he said, eyes gleaming. He leaned closer towards her, but she shifted her feet and moved out of reach.

His eyes were laughing as he opened the door for her. 'Don't look so serious,' he said. 'See you, Briana.'

When David returned on Monday he was like a different person. He was unusually quiet all day and worked hard. Briana could not help but feel rather triumphant that her tactics had succeeded. She praised his work and received a hesitant smile. 'Are you not mad at me any more?' he asked.

'Nothing to be mad about now, is there?'

He shook his head and sighed with relief. 'I'm sure glad.'

As was his normal routine, Brand came into her work room a couple of times that day, saying nothing to her but good morning or simply giving her a nod in greeting. As the weeks progressed she was becoming more and more resentful of his attention. It seemed as if his eyes were on her constantly, whether he was in the room or not. She tried hard to ignore it, but his silent surveillance was getting on her nerves. She resented his constant checking up on her and her work. Brand liked to be on top of things, which was fair enough. He did not trust her, which she found less tolerable.

Although getting used to the routine of working in the shop was tiring, she gained tremendous satisfaction from it. The work was going well. The dental equipment order had been delivered in time. The bath towels for the health club were also finished and had generated a new order for a hundred more.

Most important of all, the people liked her and opened up to her. They told her about their home life, about the things they did in their spare time. David confided that he was saving up for his own colour TV. Jill said she wanted her hair done just like Briana's and what did she think about it?

'You'll have to very, very sure. Your hair is straight so you'll need a permanent, and once you have that it won't come out for a long time. You're stuck with it whether you like it or not.'

Jill nodded thoughtfully. 'It looks so-so-so pretty.'

Jim rattled the change in his pockets and gave a wide grin. 'That's because Briana is pretty, stupid.'

Jill's dark eyes shot fire. 'I-I-I'm not stupid!'

Jim shrugged. 'All girls are stupid. My brother says so.' He glanced at Briana and flushed. 'Well, I don't mean you.' He turned hastily and went back to work. Briana couldn't suppress a smile and she winked at Jill.

'Men aren't so smart, either. Don't let Jim get to you.'

Her lunch hour was usually spent with Kathleen, the secretary and Margaret, the counsellor. As Julie had told her, both were scared stiff of Brand. They painted him as a tyrant and a slave-driver, impatient and arrogant.

This fear of Brand, however, did not keep Kathleen and Margaret from having a grudging respect for him and for the work he had accomplished. Neither did it keep them from speculating about his love life and his prowess in bed. After all, Brand was a very masculine, virile-looking specimen. It was obvious that Brand featured prominently in their fantasies and that they thought about him with a kind of fearful excitement. Brand, however, showed no interest in the women around him, which only made him more intriguing. According to the gossip there'd been a woman once, some years ago, but no one knew what had happened. There were no signs of a female in his life now. He stayed at the office for hours after the shop closed and often came back on Saturday mornings.

For three weeks running, *The Loudoun Times Mirror* sported an advertisement asking for a department supervisor for the workshop. Kathleen kept Briana advised on the applicants, who were few and far between, and according to her, all hopelessly unqualified. The fact that by all theoretical standards Briana was 'hopelessly unqualified' as well did not seem to occur to her.

Briana could not help but feel tense and defensive whenever she thought about the situation, which was too often. Everything was going so well. Apart from minor problems and frustrations, she seemed to have no great trouble running the place. However, that was her own opinion and, as such, of no importance. It was Brand's opinion that counted in the end and he was still interviewing applicants.

The lady with the silvery-blue hair she'd met at Julie's goodbye party was sitting in the pew in front of her in church a few weeks later. After the service she came up to Briana, putting her hand on her arm.

'How are you, honey? I heard you're working at the shop. It's just wonderful! You know, Brand is such a wonderful man. So patient and kind and always ready to help. He used to live across the street from me, and I could always count on him. He shovelled my drive when there was snow and when I had trouble with my hip he helped all he could. No finer man than him I always say. And to see what he has done for Billy! Billy is my grandson and he works in the shop, cutting boards in the woodshop. He's a different boy since he went there. It's a miracle, you know. We can't be more lucky than to have a good man like Brand in our community.'

Briana's smile had grown stiff on her face. 'Yes, yes, you're quite right, Mrs . . . eh . . '

'Mable. Just call me Mable. Everybody does. Well, it was so nice seeing you, honey.' And with a bright smile she turned and walked off.'

So patient and kind and always ready to help. Briana stared at the curly, silvery-blue head and wondered if they'd been thinking about the same man.

He's really a wonderful guy, once you get to know him.

Julie's words. Obviously, I haven't got to know him yet, she thought wryly. He keeps the patient, helpful, wonderful part of himself for his friends and the workers in the shop. I get the suspicion and distrust and silence. It was a bitter thought. After all those weeks of hard work, his attitude towards her had not changed. And her three months were almost up.

It was October now and the leaves were turning, the colours a beautiful mixture of gold and brown and red and orange. Grandma's chrysanthemums bloomed in a variety of colours along the front of the house. The farmers had their pumpkins out by the road, huge heaps of orange balls reminding her that Hallowe'en was coming up.

In the last few months there had been little time to do much about the house, but she had managed to empty most of the cupboards and taken boxes full of things to the church rummage sale. The furniture was still where it had always been, although she had taken down the wall plaques and other knick-knacks. In two weeks time she'd know for sure if she'd be staying here permanently. Until then it wasn't worth doing more than she had done so far.

She wondered how she was going to get through the next two weeks.

On the last day, Brand called her into his office.

'You're in luck,' Kathleen whispered. 'He's in a good mood today.'

She entered, closing the door behind her.

Brand gestured at the chair in front of his desk. 'Sit down, Briana.'

She sat down.

'Your three months are up.' He paused significantly. 'And we have not found another suitable person for the job.'

One thing she had to admire him for: he didn't beat around the bush. Straight to the point every time. She nodded, saying nothing.

He looked right at her. 'You have done an admirable job, Briana.'

She was waiting for a 'but', which did not materialise. 'Thank you.'

'I'd like to hear from you what you think about the job. Is it what you anticipated? Is it as easy or as difficult as you had expected?'

'I enjoy working here,' she said stiffly. 'I'm able to handle most of the work without trouble. It's difficult at times, of course, but I'm still learning. I like the people. I get along with them, and they seem to take to me.'

He nodded. 'I've noticed.'

She was silent.

'I believe that the best thing for the shop would be for you to stay on on a permanent basis.' It was a statement of fact, not a question, and again Briana made no comment.

He leaned back in his chair in a manner now familiar to her and gave her a penetrating look. 'Are you still interested?'

She nodded. 'Yes.'

'Thank you.'

She glanced up in surprise and she saw a glimmer of a smile curve his lips.

'I'm happy to have found someone who can do the job so well, though I must admit I never expected it to be you.'

'You'd made up your mind before I'd even opened my mouth,' she couldn't help saying.

'We all make mistakes,' he said drily.

'Even you?'

There was a glint of amusement in his eyes. 'Even I. It's not easy to admit a mistake, but I was wrong about you.'

'I'm glad I was able to convince you of that.'

'So am I.'

She couldn't figure this man out. One day he was

intolerably arrogant, now he was freely admitting to mistakes, not batting an eye.

'And now that we've settled that, how about dinner Saturday night?'

Briana practically gaped at him. This was getting better and better. 'Dinner? You're asking me to dinner? Why?'

'I do that now and then,' he said drily, 'ask a woman out to dinner.'

'But why me? You don't even like me.'

'Maybe I was wrong about that too. It seems a good idea to get to know you better now that you'll be a permanent member of the staff.'

She wondered how well he knew the other permanent members of the staff—Kathleen and Margaret. Her guess was that even at gun-point he couldn't come up with the colour of their eyes.

Briana was glad she'd asked her mother to send some of her clothes from Florida. Dinner with Brand. To what kind of place would he take her? All she ever wore to work were jeans and shirts or sweaters, covered with a work smock. The first time he'd seen her she'd worn her suit from Paris from which he'd concluded that she was a spoiled little rich girl looking for do-gooder work.

Well, she didn't care what he thought about her. She felt like dressing up—a nice dress, long earrings, high heels. She had them in her wardrobe and she was going to wear them whether he liked it or not. Ross had taken her out to dinner in Washington once, and once they'd gone to see a play at the Kennedy Center, and he had been delighted to see her in all her finery.

She took her time getting ready, choosing a simple, white lambswool dress that looked like it had cost the earth, which it probably had. Her mother had bought it for her in Italy as a present, saying it was just the thing for her. She'd loved it on sight. Jade earrings and a jade necklace looked lovely against the white and she looked in the mirror with satisfaction. It would do anywhere.

When Brand arrived, she was ready. The grey eyes ran over her in swift appraisal and she couldn't stop her heart from making some nervous little leaps at the sight of him. The lamp-light brought out the red glints in his hair like sparks of fire. He was casually dressed in brown slacks, a tweed jacket with a roll-neck sweater under it. The pipe was missing, though. She liked the relaxed, comfortable look of him.

He glanced around the room, hands in his pockets, jacket pushed back. 'Whose house is this?' he asked.

'Mine, of course.'

His eyes ran over the old-fashioned furniture, the worn carpeting, the picture by an amateur painter on the wall. 'I see.' His face gave nothing away. 'Ready to go?'

She nodded, picking up her bag and her white wool coat from a nearby chair and opened the door.

It was windy and cold outside and heavy clouds threatened rain. Brand opened the door to his Pontiac station-wagon, taking his trench coat off the seat and tossing it into the back before helping her inside. As he moved behind the steering wheel he gave her a half-amused smile. 'This car does not seem to be the appropriate vehicle to transport all this elegance. Do forgive me.'

'Would you prefer me to change into jeans?' Irritation sharpened her tone.

'Absolutely not. You look gorgeous. I'll enjoy looking at you for the rest of the evening.' He sounded amused but sincere.

'Thank you,' she said sweetly. 'And please don't be self-conscious about your car.'

'I wasn't, actually.'

'I didn't think so, actually.'

He laughed. 'All right, off we go.' He turned the key

in the ignition and the engine sputtered into action with a few asthmatic gasps. 'It's been a good car,' he commented as they swung on to the road. 'I like it because it can carry people and things by the numbers. But it is getting a little decrepit, I admit.'

He took her to a Colonial-style restaurant in Leesburg, a small place with subdued lighting and a friendly atmosphere. Long red tablecloths covered the tables, all of which were graced by a candle in a rather ornate pewter candlestick and a single carnation in a bud vase.

'What would you like to drink?' he asked her when the waitress came to take their orders.

'I'll have some tomato juice, please.'

'Something in it? Vodka?'

'Just a drop of Tabasco.'

He ordered a whiskey for himself and the waitress departed. They examined the menu, Brand selecting a steak and Briana choosing the stuffed sole.

'Would you like some wine with your dinner?' he asked, checking the wine list.

'I'd rather have some mineral water.'

He cocked one eyebrow. 'You don't drink?'

She shook her head. 'No.' It was obvious that it surprised him and it amused her a little. He had all sorts of preconceived ideas about her that were biting the dust one after the other.

'All right, Perrier for you. Do you mind if I have a glass of wine?'

'Not in the least.'

He closed the menu and put it down. 'You surprise me,' he commented conversationally.

'Why? Because I don't drink?'

'Yes. It seems . . . out of character. Why don't you?'

'Does there have to be a reason? I just don't like alcohol. I never did.'

His eyes narrowed slightly and he gave her a searching look.

Briana felt a surge of irritation. 'You don't believe me, do you? You think someone with my background probably drinks like a fish. Or maybe you think I once did and got into trouble. Well, I'm sorry to disillusion you. There's nothing sinister about it. I'm not a reformed alcoholic. And I'm sick and tired of you looking for things to disapprove of!'

'Hey, hey!' he said soothingly, but she couldn't stop herself. The patience and control she'd carefully nursed the last few months seemed suddenly to have run out. Her hand trembled and she lowered her glass to the table.

'Don't you think I know? You've been watching me like a hawk for the past three months, waiting for me to do something wrong so you can pounce on me. I'm fed up with your suspicious attitude towards me! You don't trust me! I don't even understand why I'm here with you!'

All she wanted was to get away from him. She didn't know what had got into her, how she had let herself get so carried away by her emotions. She reached for her handbag next to her chair, then let it drop back down again. Digging her nails into the palms of her hands, she took a deep breath.

She was *not* going to make a scene.

She was *not* going to let him get to her.

She was going to control herself. Now.

He watched her, saying nothing, making no apologies and the silence stretched uncomfortably.

'I think,' he said at last, 'that you're here for the same reason I am.'

'And what is that?'

His eyes held hers. 'We're curious about each other.'

CHAPTER FOUR

THE words hung between them in the silence, heavy with meaning. *We're curious about each other.* Briana felt a thrill of excitement. Was it true? Was she curious about him? He was a tough, aggressive male with a certain magnetism, a sense of power that stirred her senses and it would be foolish to deny it, although subconsciously she must have done just that ever since she'd first met him. She understood that now and the realisation that she had deceived herself to such an extent came to her with dismay. And now, in the rosy light of the candle, with his eyes still looking into hers, the implications seemed disturbing.

'Don't deny it,' he said softly.

'I'm not.' She played with her spoon, sliding her fingers along the cool, shiny metal. 'It's difficult not to be curious about a man like you.' Her voice was beautifully calm. 'There are many conflicting opinions about you in this town. Interesting, I think.'

'Is that so?' He seemed amused. He leaned back in his chair, arms folded across his chest. 'What do they say about me?'

She went on fingering the spoon, watching the contorted reflection of the candle in the rounded shape, her pause intentional. 'An old lady, Mable— you know her—told me you were so kind and patient and always ready to help.'

'And you don't think that?'

'There are a number of people who don't think that. They're of the opinion that you're a slave-driver, hard to get along with and arrogant.' By the look in his eyes she was telling him nothing he hadn't heard before.

He nodded. 'You forgot tyrannical and bad-tempered and impatient.'

'All that too.'

'You do my ego good.'

'Thank you.'

The waitress arrived with their food. For a while they ate in silence. The fish was good. Brand's appetite did not seem to have suffered from the attack on his ego and he was eating his steak with obvious pleasure.

'About you,' he said after a while, 'I've heard almost nothing.'

'Have you asked around?'

He shook his head, eyes gleaming. 'No, but our mutual friend Mable mentioned you to me just a few days ago. Said you go to church almost every Sunday.'

'I do.' She tried not to be defensive. 'Is that surprising?'

'About you, nothing surprises me any more. Did you always go to church?'

'No. Just since I came here.'

'Why?'

'I've come to the conclusion that my spiritual life needs a little attention,' she said lightly. 'Do you go to church?'

'Seldom.' There was a pause as he eyed her with interest. 'Why did you leave Florida?'

'I didn't really leave. I just came here to take care of my grandmother's affairs after she died.' She shrugged. 'Then I decided to stay.'

'You're living in your grandmother's house, then?'

'Yes.'

He gave her a long look. 'I'm sure that's not exactly the type of place you're used to living in.'

She felt her hackles rise. 'Anything wrong with it?'

'I didn't say that. Tell me about your life in Florida.'

She met his eyes. 'I thought you'd already found

out all you wanted to know.' The bitterness was hard to hide.

'Only the bare essentials.'

'That I'm a spoiled little rich girl who married a jet-setting playboy.'

'Who drowned at sea in the company of another woman he'd taken out sailing on his yacht.'

Her body tensed and she gave him a cold look. 'See? You're very well informed.'

'I don't think I am.'

'You've got all the facts straight,' she said icily.

'They don't seem to fit together very well.'

'They're perfectly true.'

'Why are you not in Florida living the life of a spoiled little rich girl? Or more to the point, a spoiled little rich widow?.'

She shrugged. 'The fun and rewards of that kind of life are highly overrated, believe me. I was tired of it. I was bored to tears with the people. I've never been much of a jet-setter. My parents aren't. My father started his own business and my mother grew up right here, in the house I live in now. They're basically very ordinary people.'

'Why then did you ever marry a guy like Cliff Crossley?'

Her wedding picture flashed before her mind's eye. She saw herself, the happy, glowing bride, and Cliff with his handsome, charming face. 'Because I loved him.' Her voice carried a note of bitterness. He hadn't deserved her love and it wouldn't be easy to ever give it again freely without the fear of what might happen.

'He hurt you badly, didn't he?'

'It was my own fault. I was a romantic—stupid, blind.' She met his eyes. 'Can we change the subject?'

'Would you care for some dessert?' he asked smoothly.

'Just coffee will be fine.'

His eyes held hers. 'I'm sorry, I shouldn't have

asked that question. Add lack of tact and insensitivity to the list of my defects.'

It was not what you'd call a charmed evening. It rained when they left the restaurant and the wind swept the masses of sodden dead leaves across the street and through the air.

'Stay here,' he ordered, pulling up the collar of his trench coat. 'I'll bring the car in front. No need for both of us to get wet.' Head bent, he hurled his big frame into the rain and she watched him disappear with long strides into the wet, swirling darkness.

The evening had not been much of a success. Part of it due to her own defensiveness and distrust. Over coffee they'd talked about the shop, a less personal subject, and about cars. He was considering buying a new car, he'd told her, keeping the Pontiac for when he needed the space.

Although the car was close by in the restaurant parking lot, Brand's face was streaming with water when he came back. She slid into the passenger seat and couldn't help laughing. The wet hair plastered to his forehead gave him a boyish, innocent look.

He cocked one eyebrow. 'What's so funny?'

'You. With your hair wet like that you don't look half as threatening as you usually do.'

'Threatening? Good Lord, the list never ends.'

'You can take it.'

'Cut me, I bleed.'

'I doubt it. If you did, you wouldn't have got the shop where it is now. No matter what people say about you, underneath they have a lot of respect for you.'

'Well, I'm glad to hear that. I was beginning to think I was a real loser.'

'I'll bet,' she said.

Soon they'd left Leesburg behind and were driving down the dark country road that would take them to her house.

'Slow down a little,' Briana cautioned as they came closer. 'The house is coming up, but it's hard to see in the dark. Before you know it you've passed it.'

'It was dark when I picked you up.'

'Right. Sorry.' She rummaged in her bag for the house key. She wasn't going to ask him in. The thought of the two of them in her small house made her uneasy.

He came to a stop in front of the house.

'Don't get out,' she said, 'you're wet enough already.' Key in hand she reached for the car door. 'Thanks very much for dinner. I'll see you on Monday.'

'Wait.' He switched on the inside light. Her hand dropped away from the door handle and she felt her body tense.

'What?'

His mouth quirked. 'Relax.'

'I'm perfectly relaxed.'

He shifted in his seat, turning towards her. 'I just wanted to tell you that I am pleased you're staying on at the shop. You're very bright and talented and you care, I know that.'

'Thank you,' she said stiffly. She didn't know what he was leading up to, but she didn't trust him for a moment.

'You're also very beautiful,' he said slowly. 'And sexy and desirable.'

She turned away. 'Spare me the admiration,' she said coolly. 'I've heard it all before.' She stared out into the dark night. The world was nothing but a black void outside the car window.

'Oh, I don't doubt it,' he said and his voice was low and mildly amused. 'I can see it all. All those poor suckers dropping at your feet and you stomping all over them.'

She gave a mocking little laugh. 'Is that the way you think it was? Please don't waste your pity on the men who were after me. They liked my looks all right. They liked my money even more.'

'Is that why your husband married you?'

'My husband was the possible exception. He had enough money of his own and my father's business didn't interest him in the least. He could have had any beautiful woman he wanted. There wasn't anything special about me.' She stopped, her hands clasped in her lap. Brand said nothing and she cast him a quick glance. He was looking at her intently and she averted her gaze.

'You're wrong,' he said at last. 'There's something very special about you, and it has nothing to do with being beautiful or being wealthy. The people in the shop care for you and they don't know anything about you, but they sense a phoney from the start and you're not one. What you give them is real. And what they give you is real.'

She nodded. 'Yes, I know. I think that's why I like this work.' The people cared about her. It was obvious in many small ways. They needed her, but she needed them too. Despite the pressure and the problems, she'd never felt more whole, more human than she had in these last few months.

'Briana?'

She met his eyes and there was warmth in them and a peculiar light. He took her hand, holding it between the two of his and leaned slightly towards her.

She sat transfixed, staring at her hand clasped between his, feeling the contact shivering through her body like a slow current of fire. It was the first time he'd ever touched her and something sprang alive deep inside her. She was suddenly overwhelmed by a curious sense of lightheadedness and it was difficult to breathe.

'Briana?' he repeated.

She raised her eyes. 'Yes?' she said huskily, aware of the erratic thumping of her heart.

'You may find this hard to believe, but I've been dreaming about you at night.'

It seemed such an improbable confession to come from a man like Brand that she was lost for words. His grey eyes looked soft in the dim light of the car and a smile tugged at the corners of his mouth.

'Are you surprised?' he asked.

'I'm not sure. It depends on the sort of dream, I suppose,' she said, instantly regretting her words. 'Were you firing me?' she added, hoping to save something. 'Did you dream you'd finally found somebody really qualified? Three relevant degrees, twenty years of experience?'

His laugh was low and amused. 'No. I was dreaming of this.' Releasing her hand, he took her face between his big hands and bent his mouth to hers. Her heartbeat throbbed in her head and a rush of sweet excitement swept over her. Her lips parted under his and he kissed her with a gentle tenderness that surprised her.

'Something like that,' he said, releasing her with a crooked smile. 'Maybe not quite so innocent. Do you approve?'

'Approve?' She looked at him, dazed.

'Of the dreams I'm having about you.'

She pulled herself together with an effort and shook her head. 'It's not a good idea.'

'Why is that?'

'I'm not on the market for dreams.'

'Is there someone else?'

She gave a dry laugh. 'No.' She opened the car door to avoid further conversation. 'Good night, Brand.'

'Good night, Briana.'

She ran quickly up to the house and went inside. He didn't drive away until she'd closed the door and turned on the lights.

She dreamed of Cliff again that night, of the time they'd returned from a party and Cliff was drunk.

'You were the most goddmaned beautiful woman at the party, you know that?' he said. 'You have class, real class. That's what I always liked about you.'

When she awoke in the morning, she remembered the words. She stared at the old dolls on the shelf, not seeing them. Maybe that's why he had married her. Because she had class, real class. She gave a bitter little laugh and swung her legs out of bed.

Something had changed. It seemed difficult to think about Brand in impersonal terms only, as she had done until then. She remembered the feel of her hand between his, the seemingly innocent kiss that had affected her more than she wanted to admit. More and more she found her thoughts occupied with him in a way that disturbed her. She wasn't ready for this. She wasn't ready for another man, for love, for trust.

After a lot of thought and deliberation, Jill had definitely decided to have her hair done in curls just like Briana's. Briana had stayed out of the discussions as much as possible, not wanting to influence Jill one way or the other.

It was a different Jill who came back to work the next day and all the women oohed and aahed over her while the men made funny cracks. Jill glowed. Brand, on his daily tour, told her she looked beautiful and the compliment made her eyes sparkle with delight.

The incident triggered a period of intense concern with physical appearance, aided by the fact that the group home was planning a party to which everyone at the shop was invited. About half the people employed in the workshop lived with parents or relatives, the other half lived in the group home, built a few years ago with funds from an anonymous benefactor. For the next week the party was the topic of conversation. Tammy was going to buy a new dress. Steve had already bought a party shirt, one with lace down the front, he explained, like the film stars on TV. Briana was asked by Georgina, one of the older women, if she would please come along to help her buy a new blouse at White's. Sally, a heavy young woman in her late twenties, mentioned for the first time that she wanted to be thin. It was Julie who had told Briana that Sally's weight problem was caused by the drugs she was taking to control her seizures.

'You can be pretty even if you're not thin' Briana said gently. 'You can't help your weight problem. Jill can't walk, Tom over there can't hear or talk. There's nothing we can do about these things.'

'I go on a diet,' Sally said stubbornly. 'I see it on TV.'

'Have you talked about it with your sister?' Sally lived with an older sister who had three kids of her own and a drunk for a husband.

'She just laugh. She fat too. She say she don't care what I do.'

'What about your doctor?'

Sally shrugged. 'He say it's them pills and he can't do nothing.'

The tragedy of Sally's joyless, loveless life tugged at Briana's heart.

'Why don't you do something else? Maybe a new hairdo. Sometimes we just want a change.' Sally's soft brown hair hung straight and shapeless around her face, the locks often hanging clear in her eyes. Briana suspected that at times her sister simply took the sewing scissors and lopped off a piece. From what Sally had told her, her sister took most of Sally's wages to help feed the family. The husband had been out of work for several months now and was seldom sober.

'Cost too much money to go to the beauty shop,' Sally said morosely, repeating probably what her sister had told her.

'Maybe I can think of something,' Briana said, not

knowing how she was going to get out of this now. Her heart ached for poor, unhappy Sally.

The easiest solution, to pay for a proper haircut for Sally herself, would not do. Giving Sally a haircut herself wouldn't be good either. Although she could improve on the present non-style, it would still not be a professional job.

Of all unlikely sources, Ross came up with the solution. 'My sister is coming to stay again for a few days. She'll do it.'

'She's a hairdresser?'

'A hair *stylist*,' he emphasised, laughter in his eyes. 'And she's good, too. I even trust her enough to let her do my hair now and then.'

Briana laughed. 'Well, in that case . . .' A plan was ripening in her head. The party at the group home was coming up next Saturday. No better excuse than a party to have your hair done. She'd have to ask Sally's sister for approval of course, but how could she refuse?

For a while she thought about how to phrase her request in the most tactful manner, then took the telephone and dialled.

She shouldn't have worried about it. Sally's sister had no objections, having problems on her mind more important than Sally's hair. Two of her kids had the chicken-pox and her husband had broken a window to get into the house the night before.

Briana hung up, letting out a heavy sigh. Was she making a mistake getting too involved in the personal life of her workers?

At lunch in the shop cafeteria next day, Brand waved her over. Carrying her tray, she weaved around tables, chairs, wheelchairs and people on crutches and looked at Brand questioningly when she reached his table in the far corner.

He pulled out a chair for her. 'Sit down.'

This was a first. If she saw him at all at lunch, he

was either alone or with one or more of the foremen from the wood shop.

She placed the tray on the table and sat down, aware of Kathleen's and Margaret's eyes on her back.

'Didn't you have breakfast this morning?' Brand enquired, examining her laden tray with raised brows.

'I did. But seven o'clock is a long time ago and I'm starving.' She picked up her spoon and began to eat her tomato soup.

'I had dinner at my parents' house last night,' he began. 'Tammy was telling me she wants to get her hair done just like yours.'

It was a statement, nothing more, but Briana could feel herself grow tense in defence. 'I didn't know that,' she said stiffly.

'Since Jill had hers done last week, Tammy hasn't stopped talking about it.'

Lowering her spoon, she met his eyes. 'It was entirely Jill's own idea. I had nothing to do with it. I didn't even encourage it.'

'I wasn't accusing you,' he said mildly.

'I get the idea you think I'm responsible.'

'Don't be so damned defensive, Briana!' His voice was low but irritated.

She didn't reply, but gripped her soup spoon tightly and brought it to her mouth. He ate his sandwich in silence.

'I think Jill looks nice with that hairdo,' she said at last, 'but Tammy . . . it's not for Tammy.' In her mind's eye, Briana saw Tammy's round face with the big blue eyes. A head full of curls and she'd look like some overgrown doll. 'I don't think it'll look right on her.'

'I don't think so either,' he said drily. 'It'll be a disaster.'

'You want me to talk to her?'

He nodded. 'I think she'll listen to you. She thinks the world of you. She keeps telling us how beautiful you are.'

Briana picked up her sandwich and didn't reply.

'What are you doing for Thanksgiving?' he asked after a pause. 'Are you going home?'

She nodded, surprised at his interest. 'And you?'

'My parents and Tammy are going to New Hampshire to my mother's sister. I've decided to stay here and have some friends over to my place for Thanksgiving dinner. I wanted to invite you in case you had no other plans.'

Briana put her sandwich down, too amazed to say a word.

He laughed softly. 'Don't look so surprised, Briana. Be open-minded. Maybe I'm not really such a hard-nosed, insensitive tyrant as you think I am. There maybe a human side to me, hidden deep inside.'

There was an open invitation in the statement, but she chose to ignore it, or at least to pretend to. She felt a fluttering of excitement and it annoyed her. What did he want from her, anyway? She took a bite from her sandwich which effectively kept her from answering. Would he do his own cooking? she wondered. Putting on a traditional Thanksgiving dinner—roasted stuffed turkey, yams, pumpkin pie and all the trimmings was a time-consuming job. Somehow she couldn't quite imagine him in the kitchen fooling with stuffings and sauces.

She swallowed her food. 'Who's doing the cooking?' she asked.

'Thinking of coming after all?'

'I can't, my mother would be destroyed. She puts on an affair you wouldn't believe.'

'I believe it,' he said drily, and she could feel immediate antagonism rear its head. By the narrowing of his eyes she could tell he had sensed her reaction. 'Doesn't every mother?' he added. 'Mine is as bad as anyone I know.'

She really would have to do something about her suspicious reactions. It was beginning to be second nature whenever she was with him. She looked down into her coffee-cup, feeling guilty.

'And to answer your question,' he continued, 'I'm doing the cooking. With a little help from my friends, that is. We're divvying up the work. I'm taking care of the turkey.'

'Ever done it before?'

He grinned. 'No, but I've got a cookbook and I can read.'

A perfect recipe for disaster, Briana thought, not without relish, but wisely refrained from saying so.

He called her to his office later that afternoon to check with her about a quote for a new job.

'Come sit over here,' he told her, pulling over a chair next to his behind the desk.

She sat down, aware of their nearness, trying to ignore it. 'What kind of job is it?'

'Folding cardboard boxes and inserting an instruction sheet. We'll get the boxes flat. All we have to do is fold them and tape them and put the paper in. It's for a company that manufactures electronic circuit boards.' His hand lay on the desk, the fingers curved around a pencil. A big, strong hand, capable of tender touches. She tore her eyes away.

'Who else is quoting?'

'I don't know. Maybe nobody. But we do have to give them an estimate. I need some information from you to see if we can handle it.' He was all business, cool and collected. She didn't feel cool and collected. She wanted to touch him, reach out and stroke his hand. It was a crazy impulse, yet she squashed it with difficulty.

She forced herself to concentrate. They discussed the job for some time, looking at figures and schedules, and came up with something that satisfied them both.

'Good,' he said, looking pleased. 'This should do.'

They both got up at the same time. They stood very close, the chair preventing her from moving aside quickly. He smiled into her eyes and the businesslike expression had vanished from his face. She was acutely aware of him, her body tingling with his nearness. Crinkly lines radiated out from the corners of his eyes. A lock of reddish hair lay over his forehead. His mouth . . . She looked away.

'I hope we'll get it,' she said, her voice not quite steady. She reached out to move the chair, but he took her hand and drew closer yet. She couldn't move, heard her heart throbbing in the stillness of the office. His free hand came up and with one finger he traced the shape of her mouth. It was such a simple, yet erotic touch that the breath caught in her throat.

'Why aren't you in the market for dreams?' he asked softly.

She closed her eyes, moving her head sideways to avoid his touch. 'I've had my share of dreams,' she said huskily.

'And they turned out to be nightmares?'

She opened her eyes and looked at him. 'Brand, please let me go.'

He shook his head, slowly sliding his arms around her drawing her fully up against him. He cradled her head and with infinite tenderness he kissed her mouth. She could feel the warmth of his body through her clothes and her senses thrilled at the contact. Oh, God, she thought, what's happening to me? I don't want this. I don't want to feel this way . . . But there was so much magic in his kiss, in the way he held her, so much sweet, wonderful delight in the feel of that strong male body against her own that she could not help responding to him.

It seemed a long time later when he finally drew back. With both hands he smoothed her hair back from her face, looking at her with a faint smile curling his mouth. 'There's always time for another dream,' he said softly.

*   *   *

Marianne was more than willing to help with Sally's hair. She'd brought all her paraphernelia with her and refused the payment Briana offered.

Sally was excited at having her hair done and she was already waiting at the gate when Briana arrived at her house to pick her up on Saturday morning.

She was wearing dark blue trousers that were too tight and too short, and a pink nylon turtleneck sweater under a frayed quilted jacket of army green. Sockless feet stuck into worn sneakers, exposing bare ankles. Briana's heart contracted. Her impulse was to drive her straight to White's in town and buy her some clothes that fitted. She wondered with a sinking heart what Sally would wear to the party tonight. It had never been mentioned. Maybe she did have something that satisfied her. After all, that was all that mattered. She didn't have to look pretty or fashionable by society's standards, as long as she herself felt comfortable in the clothes she wore.

Sally looked with big eyes at Marianne's tools spread out on the kitchen table. 'Like a real beauty shop,' she concluded. Marianne set to work, talking to Sally all the time, making jokes. Briana kept little Bobby entertained and peeked in now and then to see the progress.

Marianne took her time. When it was all over and Sally's hair was blown dry, Briana was amazed at the difference.

'And it's very easy, you know,' Marianne told Sally. All you do is wash it, comb it with the parting here, and let it dry. You don't even need a hairdryer.'

Sally stared at herself in the mirror in utter delight. 'I look . . . I look pretty,' she stammered.

'You do. And I'll tell you what. You give me your phone number and I'll let you know when I come again, so we can keep it up. How's that?'

Sally looked away from the mirror. 'You will? Really?'

'Sure. It's fun, I cut all my friends' hair. I like making people pretty.'

'You're nice,' Sally said, glowing. 'One of the nicest people I know.'

Briana heard a car come up the drive and a few moments later there was a knock on the front door. Brand. It was the last person Briana expected on a Saturday morning, and seeing the broad-shouldered figure looming over her as she opened the door made her heart give a giant leap. Oh, God, she thought, this is ridiculous.

He smiled down at her. 'Hello, Briana.'

'Hi. Come in.'

When he stepped into the living room, Sally entered from the kitchen and her face broke out in a wide smile. 'Mr Edwards! Look at my hair!'

Briana moaned inwardly, remembering the lunch-time conversation about his sister's hair. He would probably think she was conspiring to change everybody's hairstyle. His expression gave nothing away, but she couldn't help feeling uneasy. Thank God that at least she'd been able to convince Tammy to leave her hair alone.

Brand looked from Sally to Briana and then back at Sally.

'You look beautiful, Sally.'

Sally beamed. 'It's for the party tonight. Marianne do it. She in the kitchen.'

'Hi.' Marianne materialised in the room. Briana made introductions. She wondered why Brand was here, but she couldn't very well ask him right out. He was talking to Marianne, who, with her easy-going manner, had no problem talking to anybody.

'How about some coffee?' she asked. 'I just made a fresh pot.' If Brand was in a hurry he'd come to the point and leave.

Apparently he was not in a hurry. They all went back to the kitchen, where Briana poured the coffee and cut up a walnut-apple cake she'd made the night before. It was an elegant-looking affair, pretty enough for a cookbook picture.

'Is this another one of your luscious creations?' Brand asked.

She nodded. 'Yep.'

'You should be doing my turkey instead of me.' He gave a lopsided grin. 'Step one and I'm already lost.'

'What's step one?'

'Buying the turkey. I was at the supermarket this morning to buy the beast and when I looked at the assortment I hadn't a clue as to what kind or size to get. I don't want it so big I'll be eating leftovers till January, but I want to make sure I have enough. So I thought I'd stop by and see if you had any idea.'

'How many people did you invite?'

'Ten, plus myself is eleven.'

'It takes about a pound per serving, so . . .'

'A pound? Who eats a pound of turkey?'

'Probably nobody. But you have to account for the weight of the bones and the fat that melts away.'

He frowned. 'Yes, of course.' Then he glowered at Marianne who had trouble containing her laughter. 'Don't laugh at me. You should admire me for my efforts.'

Marianne's eyes grew wide and innocent. 'Oh, I do! Tremendously!'

Briana admired him too. It was an act of great courage to take on what he was planning to do. However, she didn't believe for a moment that Brand was going to pull off that turkey dinner.

Monday morning at work Briana listened to the excited story about the group home party which apparently had been a great success. Everybody liked Sally's hair. Her sister had lent her a caftan with embroidery around the neckline and that, too, had been a success.

'She looked like a queen,' said Jim with a big grin, jingling the change in the pockets of his overalls. To hear Jim say something so positive about a female was a real surprise and Briana smiled at him approvingly. He grew faintly reddish and bent down to his work.

Later in the morning Brand called and asked to see her in his office.

'There's something I want to discuss with you,' he said.

'How do you stuff a turkey?' she guessed.

He frowned. 'Turkey? Oh, no. This is work.'

He was his serious, businesslike self again and Briana sighed. She liked him a lot better when he was more relaxed and in a lighter frame of mind.

'What is it?' She was beginning to feel edgy and his frown made her stiffen in defence.

'It's about Sally.'

There we go, she said silently. Stoically she stared at him.

'I appreciate what you did for her, but I think you should be careful.'

'Careful about what?'

'About interfering in other people's lives.'

'I wasn't interfering,' she said coldly. 'I was involved, maybe, but I wasn't interfering.'

He shrugged. 'Semantics.'

'Oh, for God's sake! It was nothing!'

He tapped a pencil on his desk. 'Maybe, maybe not. But for your own sake it's better not to get involved too much outside of work.'

'Sally is a special case.'

'They're *all* special cases. That's exactly why. You can't take on all their problems. You can't solve them all.'

'I'm not *trying* to!'

'Briana, don't be so damned stubborn! Your job is here, at the shop. It's a very demanding job. I know you take work home at nights sometimes, I also know that you went shopping with Georgina to help her buy something to wear for the party. If you start involving yourself with the employees outside of work hours you'll be taking on too much. There's never an end to it. Believe me, I know. I've been there. You need time for yourself.'

'I can take care of myself,' she said angrily.

'That's what *I* thought,' he said drily. 'The first few years after I opened the shop I did everything. I took the men out to football games. I took everybody to the movies, because if I didn't, nobody did. I organised parties. I tried to solve their problems by talking to parents and guardians and counsellors and doctors. I was so involved with them and their lives, I didn't have a life of my own. The cost of that was too high and I learned it the hard way.'

Something in the tone of his voice told her that it had been a painful lesson. For a moment his eyes looked strangely bleak. Was it a woman? she wondered. Maybe he hadn't given her enough of his time and attention, at least not enough to make her happy. No woman she knew liked to come second to a man's work, no matter how important or unselfish the work. The shuttered look on his face kept her from voicing the questions.

'I'll think about it,' she said, pushing her chair back and standing up. 'If there's nothing else I'd like to go now. I'm expecting a call from Richmond.'

'Go ahead.'

She turned and opened the door.

'By the way,' he said as she was about to leave the room, 'how *do* you stuff a turkey?'

She faced him with a sudden smile. 'I'd show you if I could. How about asking your mother?'

He sighed. 'I think I'll have to.'

Ross asked her to share a De Luxe pizza with him that night and she was glad for the opportunity to get out of the house. Her social life was almost non-existent, and had it not been for Ross's occasional invitations to share a pizza or go to a play in Washington, she might never leave the house at all. He had made a few attempts to bring romance to their friendship, but Briana had made it clear she was not interested.

Saturday was a gorgeous autumn day, the sky a brilliant blue, the air cool and crisp and full of the pungent fragrance of pine and dry leaves and moist soil.

In the afternoon Briana did some grocery shopping and afterwards decided on impulse to take a leisurely walk through town. It was too nice a day to stay indoors. The sun felt good on her face and she took deep breaths of the crisp air as she walked along King Street. For about an hour she browsed around in the little shops in the town centre. The Chinese carpets in the window of the carpet shop drew her attention. The pale, subtle colours were beautiful. A carpet like that belonged on a wooden floor. She wondered what was hidden under the old carpeting in Grandma's living room; pine floorboards probably. If they were any good, she could sand them down and stain them.

As she walked back to the parking lot, she redid the house in her mind, buying a Chinese carpet for the living room, cosy furniture, a wooden table to replace the formica-topped one in the kitchen. There wasn't much she wanted from her apartment in Florida. The furniture had been Cliff's—a lot of chrome and glass and cold marble. All very expensive, tasteful, modern designer stuff. All very angular, cold and without character. She'd never felt quite comfortable with it. The place looked like something out of a showroom or a glossy magazine—unreal, as if nobody actually lived in it.

I'm going to get rid of it all, she thought as she unlocked the car and got in. There was no reason to hang on to the left-overs of her married life. Briefly she leaned her head on the steering wheel, taking a deep breath. Two years of her life wasted. She'd known happiness, disillusionment, humiliation and utter despair. It was all over now, even the pain—most of it, anyway. But the memories were still there.

CHAPTER FIVE

THE happenings of that fatal afternoon were stored in her memory like a filmstrip. Sometimes it would play itself out in her mind and she could not turn it off. Every detail of that afternoon, the most painful as well as the most insignificant, were preserved with perfect clarity.

She remembered laughing that afternoon. Lunch with her friend Michelle at Zarbo's. Shopping for a sexy nightgown, shoes, a silly hat. Buying Godiva chocolates. She sang as she drove home through the hot Miami streets, feeling happy, planning dinner, anticipating Cliff's face when he saw the flimsy new black bed thing—not a nightgown, but something much more naughty and seductive.

She parked the car in the underground garage and gathered up the various packages and bags from the back seat. Clutching them to her chest she made her way to the elevator, her footsteps sounding hollow in the cavernous building. Once inside the elevator, one of the plastic bags began to slip from her grasp, then the whole lot dropped at the feet of a disapproving-looking old gentleman with shiny black shoes and equally shiny grey hair. Offering apologies, she gave him her brightest smile as she quickly bent down to gather up her purchases. Picking up one bag at the wrong end, the shimmery black outfit fell to the floor and she hastily grabbed it and stuffed it back in the bag, smiling wider. The man frowned and looked away. Had Michelle been with her, Briana knew they'd have dissolved in girlish laughter. Sour old goat, she thought, straightening up, the smile not fading from her face. He wasn't going to spoil her mood. The elevator stopped and he followed her out.

At her door she clumsily searched for her keys and the bags slipped again and landed on the floor with soft bumps and rustlings of paper and plastic. The old man passed her, eyes sliding coolly and disdainfully over her as she stood ankle deep in carrier-bags and boxes. What was a woman with such a lack of class and grace doing in a place like this? she could hear him think. Chuckling to herself she entered the apartment, tossing the packages on a chair.

Kicking off her strappy green sandals, she went into the kitchen for a glass of water. The white tiles felt cool on her warm feet. The window offered a panoramic view of Miami and she saw the haze of summer heat shimmer over the city. Inside it was comfortably cool in the perfectly controlled air-conditioned atmosphere. As she stood looking out over the city, drinking her water, she heard the vague stirrings of someone else in the apartment. The sound was coming from the bedroom. It must be Cliff, home early as he sometimes was.

'Cliff?' She opened the bedroom door, wondering why it was closed.

Cliff was standing by the bed, bare-chested, wearing jeans. On the bed, sheet clutched to her chest, lay a girl with long blonde hair and wide baby-blue eyes. Sunlight filtered through the white curtains, colouring the suntanned girl a dusky gold. In the second before shock hit her, she noticed the colours, the details. There was a wine bottle and two glasses on the bedside table. Clothes lay hastily discarded on the floor, flashes of bright colour on the soft white carpeting. Red panties and bra, violet shorts and top. Frozen, Briana stared at the girl on the rumpled bed, feeling the very life drain out of her until she was shaking with a terrifying weakness.

It was like something from a bad movie: the

unsuspecting wife coming home to find her husband in the bedroom with an empty-headed blonde—a slapstick flick that had the people rolling in the aisles. She felt her heartbeat drumming in her head, throbbing until it seemed to fill the silent room. For a fleeting moment she was outside herself, seeing the three of them, paralysed with shock, staring at each other. *Portrait of Betrayal*—a human still-life fixed in time, fixed in her mind.

Then she screamed, shattering the silence, lunging at Cliff to beat him, hit him, hurt him. Losing all reason, she hurled herself at him like a demented animal, feeling nothing but agonizing pain and primitive fury.

When sanity returned she found herself on the floor in a heap, sobbing wildly. When exhaustion overwhelmed her, she lay still, eyes closed, wanting nothing but to die.

There was silence in the apartment. Raising herself up on one elbow, she surveyed the room. The bright-coloured clothes were no longer on the floor. The girl was gone. She listened closely. Nothing. Not a sound. Cliff was gone too.

Slowly she got to her feet and went into the bathroom. Her face shocked her. She looked ravaged. Her hair stood out in all directions, her eyes looked dead like a ghost's. She'd aged ten years. Aimlessly she walked around the apartment, forcing herself to go back into the bedroom and look at the bed. *Her* bed. Her first impulse was to pack her suitcase and leave, never come back. Then from somewhere a spark of rebellion began to flicker. This was *her* bed, *her* home. She was not going to be chased out of it by some cheap blonde with red underwear.

She began to strip the bed, tearing at the sheets and mattress pad in a blinding rage. She turned the king-size mattress, which was no small job and was accomplished only with the strength of fury and determination. Bundling the sheets and mattress cover into a large plastic garbage bag, she tossed them down the garbage chute.

As she was making up the bed with clean sheets, she heard Cliff come back into the apartment. Her heart began to hammer wildly. *Stay calm*, she admonished herself. *It doesn't matter any more. It's too late.*

Cliff entered the bedroom, raising his eyebrows as he saw her. 'You're home,' he said, as if he was surprised to find her there. He leaned casually against the doorjamb, lean and tanned, blue eyes strangely bright.

Briana tossed a pillow back on the bed and faced him. If he wanted her gone, he could tell her so. She wasn't going to run.

'This is *my* home. I am your *wife*, and this is *our* bed.' She did not recognise her own voice. 'I don't care what you do outside these doors, but don't you ever, *ever* again bring another woman into this bed.'

He shrugged. 'It was about time something exciting happened here.'

Her throat went dry. 'What do you mean?' Her voice quivered with a terrible tension.

He looked at her coldly. 'You're lousy in bed, you know. You bore me to tears.'

It was as if the breath had been taken from her. The words, like jagged strips of glass, dug into her, sharp and cold as ice. She stared at him, stunned, the words echoing in her head. *You're lousy in bed, lousy in bed, lousy in bed.*

'Get out!' she whispered hoarsely. 'Get out!'

He straightened away from the doorjamb. 'Don't worry, I'm going. I just came back for my wallet.' He picked it up from his dresser and shoved it into his back pocket. 'Just you remember that *this* is *my* apartment and I bring into it anyone I damn well please.' With that parting shot he turned, walked out and slammed the front door.

*   *   *

She didn't know what happened to the rest of the afternoon, or the night. The hours passed without her being aware of it. She sat on the sofa feeling stunned and empty. No emotion, nothing. Darkness inside. The phone rang and she didn't pick it up, hearing the ringing only on the edge of her consciousness. She forgot to eat and drink and eventually fell asleep on the sofa.

The sun shining on her face woke her the next morning. She felt sick and faint with hunger and forced herself to eat some toast and drink a cup of tea. Cliff had not returned last night. She went into the bedroom and looked in his closet and drawers. His clothes were all there. She could not remember him leaving after she'd attacked him. That time was a blank. She'd lost her senses and she began to tremble remembering it. It was frightening to think it had happened to her, this total loss of reason and sanity. She could have killed him had she had a weapon. It was what she had wanted to do in that blind fury of despair.

She took a deep breath. No more. No more emotion. Nothing worse could ever happen to her. Her love, her marriage, destroyed in a second. This was it. She was going to play it cool from now on, like all those other women with their artificial smiles and empty faces. She was not alone. It had happened to countless others. She'd been naive to think the dream could go on for ever. Now nothing mattered any more. She felt dead inside.

The day passed in a blur. She sat in a chair and stared into nothingness while the hours went by. Now and then she'd get up to perform some meaningless task—straightening the black silk throw pillows on the white sofa, empty an almost-empty waste basket.

Late in the afternoon she heard a key in the lock. Cliff? She didn't care. She watched the door as it opened, feeling anaesthetised. Nothing would touch her. With cold detachment she noticed the roses, a mass of them, big, beautiful red roses. Never before had he brought her flowers other than white ones, to match the black and white décor of the apartment.

He advanced into the room, holding out the roses to her. 'I want to apologise for yesterday,' he said.

She didn't want the flowers. She wanted nothing from him, not even his apology. No apology would ever wipe out the damage he had done to her yesterday. She said nothing.

'I bought you a present,' he went on, still holding out the roses to her. With his free hand he fished in his pocket and took out a long narrow jeweller's box. He tossed it into her lap. 'I'll go put these in water.' He made for the kitchen and Briana stared at the box in her lap.

She could not believe this was happening. Cliff was trying to make up as if all they'd had was a mere squabble, a silly argument. Out of curiosity, she opened the box. A diamond necklace glittered on the blue velvet. Did he truly think he could buy off his guilt with this? He had destroyed her love and he imagined he could buy it back with red roses and the cold glitter of diamonds. But nothing could ever do that. Not even the light of sparkling diamonds could chase out the darkness inside her.

Cliff came back into the room and placed the flowers on the black marble coffee table. 'Do you like it?' he asked, motioning at the necklace.

'It's very beautiful,' she said coolly. This was not the man she had married, this empty, shallow person. This side of him she'd never seen before.

He sat down next to her on the sofa and put his arm around her shoulders. She stiffened, moving slightly.

'Briana?'

She eyed him with cold indifference. 'What?'

'It didn't mean anything, what happened yesterday.'

She suppressed a laugh. Not to him, maybe. To her it had meant everything. 'I see.' She gave him a quick, sideways glance, wondering what was going on in that handsome head. He looked like a little boy who'd lost his dog.

'You're my woman, Briana,' he said emphatically, 'and you always will be. Suzie means nothing to me, I swear.'

'Why did you bring her here?' Strangely, what she felt now was merely objective curiosity. It seemed strange that he could have done such an indiscreet, stupid thing as to bring that girl up here while she could have come home any moment.

'You said you were going shopping yesterday afternoon. You said you wouldn't be home until at least five.'

She'd come home more than an hour earlier. They'd cut their shopping spree short because Michelle had had to go to the airport to pick up her mother who'd suddenly decided to pay a visit.

Cliff jumped up restlessly, pacing the floor, hands in his pockets. 'Listen, the Romanos invited us out to dinner at La Mirabella. Richard clinched a million-dollar deal, rather unexpectedly, and he's inviting everybody to come and celebrate.'

'Fine. What time?'

He gave her a charming smile, which she interpreted as relief. She wondered why it mattered. He could have easily made up some excuse for her absence if she'd refused to go. A headache, a virus, anything. It was strange how she suddenly looked at him with totally different eyes, examining him from a different angle.

'Eight o'clock. I'll need a snack. I didn't have much lunch. Can I get you something?'

The considerate husband. How touching. 'No thank you,' she said politely.

Cliff drank too much at the party, which was not

something he did often. Briana drove home while Cliff slumped in the passenger seat beside her, talking and laughing boisterously.

'You were the most goddamned beautiful woman at the party, you know that? You have class, real class. That's what I always liked about you. Not like that Romano bitch and her loud mouth and that idiotic dress she was wearing with her boobs hanging out. And that pinched-faced Vivian. I swear she's as frigid as a frozen chicken.' He laughed out loud, apparently finding humour in his own words.

Briana stared straight ahead at the road, letting him ramble on, trying not to listen. She'd moved through the evening like a machine, smiling and talking mechanically and laughing politely when required. It had not been difficult. Having switched off all feeling, she'd continued on automatic with an ease that almost surprised her. I'm in shock, she thought. Maybe that's it.

She tried not to think about anything when she slid between the sheets after they came home. Cliff joined her on the big bed and she moved over to her own side as far away from him as possible. He shifted over towards her, wrapping himself around her. She stiffened, lying still and rigid, praying he would leave her alone.

'I love you,' he whispered in her ear.

Mentally she braced herself against the impact of the words. Cheap, cheap, she thought to herself. He didn't love her. He had no understanding of the meaning of the word love.

'I'm tired,' she said. 'I'd like to sleep now.'

He sighed. 'God, yes, me too.' He kissed her neck. 'Good night, baby.' He rolled away and relief flooded her. Her body relaxed. Still, sleep took a long time coming. Next to her Cliff lay asleep, his regular breathing the only sound in the dark, silent room. She felt no love, no hate, only indifference.

* * *

It took more than two weeks before he attempted to make love to her again. Every night she'd braced herself for the inevitable, dreading his touch. *You're lousy in bed, lousy in bed, lousy in bed*, a refrain that sang constantly in her mind as she lay rigid on the edge of the big bed. She had no idea what it was he wanted from her. She'd loved him, given freely of herself, feeling no inhibitions. She'd initiated and participated in the silly love games they sometimes played. Giving and taking equally, she'd never been a passive bed mate.

All that was over now. She could never really make love to him again. When he came to her she did not resist, but lay passive in his arms, staring at the ceiling, praying for it to be over. He tried frantically to arouse her, but did not say a word when his attempts were unsuccessful. In the end he took her in a frenzy of frustration, rolled away from her and went to sleep without even saying good night.

There were more repeats of the incident, always with the same results. She was dead inside and was incapable of feeling anything. In the day time they were polite to each other. For a while he made various attempts to restore their relationship to what it had been before—full of laughter and fun and joy. 'You never laugh any more,' he complained once.

'I don't feel like it.'

He stared at her for a long time. 'You'll never forgive me, will you?' There was anger and frustration in his eyes. 'One mistake, and it's all over. Did you expect me to be goddamned *perfect*?'

She shrugged. 'Not perfect, but trustworthy at least.' She turned and walked out of the room.

The weeks went by and she never cried, not until two months later. It started a flood of despair that went on for weeks. Every day she cried until there were no more tears. A depression settled over her, blurring the days into a grey wasteland and the crying eventually stopped. She stayed in bed for hours, staring at nothing. Cliff stayed away from her, didn't come home for days sometimes. He was seeing another woman, she knew. She didn't care. He hardly talked to her at all any more. The last time he'd tried to make love to her, he'd given up in disgust, calling her a frigid bitch.

How life continued she had no idea. Months went by and nothing happened. Sometimes she wondered vaguely why Cliff hadn't told her to leave, why she wasn't leaving herself. Why was she staying on?

Her parents were worried about her. They had guessed something terrible was wrong and had offered any help they could. But Daddy, with all his love and all his money, could not repair or replace what was broken now. She could have moved back in; they would welcome her with open arms, but something kept her from this final act of walking out on her marriage. In moments of lucidity she realised she was holding on to something that wasn't even there anymore. There was no love, no marriage. Why couldn't she make herself pack up and leave a hopeless situation? Was it pride? Could she not, even now, admit she had made a mistake, married the wrong man, a man without substance or character? I must be deranged, she thought at times. No sane woman hangs on like this.

One day, a hurricane, weakened to a tropical storm, moved in from the South where it had ravaged several Caribbean islands. It battered the Florida coast, causing damage to houses, boats and vegetation. Watching the scenes of destruction on the television news, she wondered fleetingly if Cliff's yacht had been spared the onslaught of the storm. Since he hadn't been home for days she had no way of knowing.

Two days later, two policemen came to the door and asked to speak to her. Was her husband home? When

was the last time she'd seen him? Had he gone out
sailing? Was anyone with him? What make was his
yacht?

She answered as best as she could. No, her husband
was not home. He'd been gone for five days, which
was not unusual. She did not know where he was. She
did not know whether he'd gone sailing, but since
there'd been a storm watch, surely he wouldn't have.
If he'd been with anyone, she didn't know, but it was
certainly possible. She described the yacht for them.

There was a young woman missing, they told her.
Her name was Cassie Dalton. She'd last been seen in
Cliff's company. She'd told a friend she was going
sailing. She'd been missing for four days. They had
reason to believe she was with Cliff Crossley. At the
marina the chaos caused by the storm had prevented
them from finding conclusive evidence why the boat
was gone. It could have been swept out to sea in the
storm. Cliff could have taken it out before the storm
hit, then been caught in it unexpectedly and been
unable to return to the marina.

They tried to be as kind as possible, but the picture
was clear. It was very possible that Cliff and the girl
Cassie had been caught in the storm and drowned at
sea.

Several weeks went by and Cliff did not return, and
neither did the girl. Eventually wreckage of his yacht
was washed ashore. They came to talk to her again, the
same two men. More used to emotional outbursts of
grief, they were uncomfortable with her calm
composure.

After they left she went into the bedroom and
looked at the king-size bed. It was all over now. She
didn't even have to leave. She felt no pain, no sadness,
not even relief.

CHAPTER SIX

THE Monday before Thanksgiving she woke up late and ran out of the house without breakfast. By the time she'd arrived at the shop she had a blazing headache. She stared at the empty coffee can and realised she'd forgotten to bring more coffee. She always had a pot going in her office and she wondered for a fleeting moment if she would survive the morning, let alone the day.

To make her misery complete, Jill's mother called and reported that her daughter had a terrible cold and couldn't come in to work, and probably wouldn't be back until after the Thanksgiving weekend. Briana pressed a hand against her aching forehead. Jill was supposed to finish a job today. It *had* to be done today. Someone else, then. Tammy? What was Tammy doing? God, she needed coffee. Some aspirin. Something to eat. She wasn't used to going without breakfast. Maybe she could beg something in the cafeteria kitchen.

Just as she was about to go, Kathleen stuck her head around the door. 'The big boss wants to see you pronto.' She grimaced apologetically. 'He's in an ugly mood.'

'Great,' Briana returned coldly. 'So am I.' She stomped out of the room.

Brand didn't even ask her to sit down when she entered his office. His face was all hard angles and his eyes held not a glimmer of pleasantry. She felt a shiver of foreboding. Good God, what was the matter?

'You finished an order last week for the Payne Company?' he began. 'Assembling a little gismo that goes into carpet cleaning machines?'

'Yes.'

'Did you check the work before you sent it off?'

She clenched her jaws in an effort to control herself. '*Of course* I checked it,' she said as calmly as she could. 'I check every little thing that leaves my room. And I haven't had any complaints.'

'Well, you have now,' he said coldly.

Her heart sank into her shoes. 'What do you mean?'

'The entire order was done wrong. Something about a little metal pin shoved in upside down.'

She frowned in exasperation. 'We did it the way it was supposed to be done!'

'Did you read the instructions?'

'Of course I read the instructions! What do you take me for?'

'I suggest you read them again. The order is coming back this afternoon. It will have to be done over again.'

She felt suddenly alarmingly dizzy. She sat down in a chair. There was no way she could take on any extra work. And how could she possibly have misread the instructions? She didn't even remember them as being particularly difficult. It was such a simple job. How was she going to get the whole order done again? There was hardly time to do the work that was on the present schedule.

He was tapping a pencil on the desk, looking infuriatingly superior. 'I'd like to remind you that service and quality control are major priorities. The Payne Company is one of our oldest customers and we can't afford . . .'

She got up out of the chair and glared at him. Her knees were shaking precariously. 'So, I did it, didn't I?' she said, her voice low and husky with restrained anger. 'I fouled up. It's what you were waiting for all this time, wasn't it? I hope you're happy.' She turned and marched out the door, slamming it behind her.

Her head throbbed and for a moment she leaned

against the wall to collect her sanity. First things first. Aspirin. Coffee. Food in her stomach. The girls in the kitchen looked at her curiously when she entered, stopping for a moment in their work. Their hair was tucked away under colourful shower-cap type bonnets and they wore pink aprons. They were all mildly retarded and were being trained in the cafeteria kitchen to work in restaurant kitchens. They washed and chopped vegetables, cleaned pots and pans, opened cans and helped assemble salads and desserts under the directions of Mrs Townsend, a diminutive woman of sixty who had the energy of a teenager.

'What's wrong, hon?' she exclaimed in genuine concern when she saw Briana. 'You look washed out!'

'I didn't have any breakfast and I have a splitting headache. I wonder if I could have a cup of coffee and something to eat. I'll pay for it.'

'Sit, sit,' Mrs Towsend ordered, pulling out a stool. 'How about some scrambled eggs and toast?'

Briana nodded. 'Fine, thank you.'

One of the girls was set to scrambling eggs, another to making toast. A cup of coffee appeared in front of her. She looked around while she sipped the hot brew. One of the girls was chopping onions. Another was shredding lettuce into a huge stainless steel basin. Nine o'clock and they were well into preparing lunch. On the counter in front of her stood a can with a plain white label. *Donated by the US Department of Agriculture for Food-Help Programs. Not to be Sold or Exchanged.* It contained six pounds of peaches. On a shelf over the counter similar cans stood lined up— beef, pork, peanuts, oatmeal, raisins and prunes, all in large quantities.

With some food in her stomach she felt energy returning. She swallowed some aspirin. With her brain fortified she hoped she could face the crisis better. Another cup of coffee in her hand, she made her way back to her workroom. Having satisfied herself that no one needed help at the moment, Briana went into her office to look in her files for the instructions for the Payne Company order.

She examined the illustration, read the accompanying words. The little pin had a red dot on one end. It was that end that had to be protruding out of the hole of the main part of the thing. But the illustration was misleading, for whatever that was worth. It was easy to see how she had made the mistake. Still, it was a mistake. She should have been more careful reading the words that had explained the simple illustration.

She took a deep breath, trying not to let despair swamp her. Three thousand little pins had to be pulled out of three thousand little holes and pushed back in the other way. And that while all her workers were busy with other orders and Jill was sick at home and probably wouldn't be in until next Monday.

Through the open office door she surveyed the work room. Sally had worked on the order before. She was now collating advertising leaflets. Maybe that could wait until next week . . . If she took a box of the things home she could get a good deal done at night. Frantically her brain began to work out the details.

She couldn't remember having had a worse day. Her headache had refused to leave her. The sight of the boxes full of three thousand little assembled parts had made her feel sick. It was six-thirty when she got into her car to go home.

The phone was ringing as she entered the kitchen and she rushed to pick it up. It was her mother, sounding excited.

'Briana, where have you been? I've been calling you for the last hour!'

'I was at the shop, Mom.' She rubbed her forehead. 'Don't you get off at five?'

'That's the idea, but there was a lot of work today.'

'You're not working too hard are you?'

'I'm fine, Mom, really.' It was hard to keep the irritation out of her voice.

'Listen, about Thanksgiving. We've had to change plans. Dad has to go to Tokyo. He'd planned to go next week, but something came up so he's leaving tomorrow. He'll have to be there for a while so I decided to go with him and I want you to come too. I've already got tickets. It'll do you good.'

Briana let out a hysterical little laugh. 'Mom, I can't! I have a job!'

'Well, can't you get a few days off? You've got a four-day week-end. Add a couple of days and you have a week.'

Briana's eyes settled on the box sitting on the kitchen table. 'There's no way in the world, Mom. I'm up to my ears in work. You go to Tokyo with Dad and have a good time. I'll stay here.'

'But what about Thanksgiving?' her mother wailed. 'You'll be alone!'

'I have another invitation,' she answered, remembering it was actually true. Brand had asked her. Such irony. She wouldn't go now, not in a million years. She'd rather spend the entire Thursday fitting pins into holes than go to Brand for a turkey dinner he'd probably ruin anyway. 'I'm sure it still stands,' she lied.

'Are you sure?' Her mother sounded agonized. 'I mean, I could stay home and we could have Thanksgiving together and I could fly to Tokyo on Friday. I've got everything ready, you know, the turkey and . . .'

'No, please, don't, Mom! I'll be fine! Don't worry about it. And we'll have Christmas soon.'

'Yes . . . yes,' she said with hesitation. 'If you're sure . . .'

'I'm very sure. Have a good time. Give my love to Dad.'

After she hung up, Briana stared fixedly at the old-fashioned black and red pattern of the linoleum, forcing tears back.

Well, she thought bitterly, at least I'll have all the time in the world to stick these damned pins into those damned holes.

But it wasn't so easy to keep her emotions under control. As she sat in the living-room, TV on, prying pins loose and putting them back in, tears welled up in her eyes. No turkey dinner. She'd been looking forward to being home for Thanksgiving, seeing her parents again and leaving work behind for a few days. She wiped at her eyes. She couldn't see a blasted thing with her eyes all misted over. She was going to go stark raving mad doing this three thousand times over. She got up, stretching, wincing at the pain in her head. In the kitchen she poured another cup of coffee and was just about to go back into the living-room when she heard someone coming around the house. Probably Ross, she thought, and opened the door to find him standing there with a glass jar in his hand. The jar contained a thick, creamy mixture and he put it on the table with a flourish.

'*Voilà*,' he said, 'my very own eggnog. I made a gallon of the stuff to take home on Thursday. I thought we'd try it out tonight.' He frowned, eyeing her intently. 'You look like hell. What's wrong?'

'I'm tired, I have a rotten headache that won't quit, and I'm redoing an order I screwed up.'

He whistled. 'What went wrong?'

'We stuck little pins upside down into little holes. I didn't read the instructions well enough.' She sighed. 'We got the whole batch back and I'm doing them again myself because we haven't got time at the shop.'

'Can I help?'

'You'd go batty within ten minutes.'

He grinned and patted the top of the jar. 'I brought help. Fortified with eggnog we can do anything.'

'I don't drink, Ross.'

He gave her a wide-eyed look. 'Not even *eggnog*?'

'Especially not eggnog. Imagine what it would do to me! The stuff is loaded with whiskey and rum. One glass would knock me out for a week. I'm not used to anything.'

He looked so disappointed that she almost felt sorry for him. 'Oh, well, what the heck. Let me try some of the stuff. But only a little, all right?'

He frowned. 'I don't want to lead you on to the wrong path,' he said melodramatically.

She grimaced, giving a light shrug. 'The right path hasn't done me much good lately, so let's live dangerously.'

He moved into action immediately, pouring each of them a glass, hers only half-full. 'You have any nutmeg?'

'Sure.' She found it for him and he sprinkled some on the drinks and handed her her glass.

'Now, just *sip* it, okay? Don't gulp it down.'

She couldn't help laughing. 'Don't you worry, I won't gulp it down.'

She took a careful sip.

'What do you think?' he asked eagerly.

'Sweet and creamy,' she answered. 'And full of booze.'

'It's not *that* bad!'

Bad enough, she wanted to say, but didn't. But she did like the delicate, creamy flavour. She took another sip. Maybe the alcohol would relax her enough to make the headache go away, you could never tell.

'Okay,' said Ross, 'let's get to work. Where is the stuff?'

'In the living-room.'

He followed her in, grimaced as he saw all the little plastic bags that held the individual assembled parts, and took another sip of his drink. 'Tell me what to do.'

They sat on the floor, the big box in between them and the drinks beside them and set to work. After an hour she was amazed to see how many they had done. It was so much easier with someone else to help, someone to talk to while you were working, keeping the boredom at bay. She had slowly, carefully, sipped the eggnog and was feeling fine. She felt more relaxed than she had all day and the headache was almost gone.

She looked at Ross, the shiny blond hair and the firm square chin. He didn't mind helping her do this monotonous, repetitive job, even made fun of it, clowning around while he was at it. Still, he worked fast and carefully. He looked up as if he felt her regard and there was warmth in the brown eyes.

'How's your headache?'

'It's getting better.' She smiled at him. 'Must be your miracle potion.'

'Would you like a little more?'

She hesitated. 'I'm not sure.'

He grinned. 'You're still as sober as a cabbage. Don't worry about getting drunk.'

'All right then, just a little. Let's take a break. I'll find us something to eat. I have some nuts somewhere.'

It was well after ten when they finally gave up. 'I'll leave the eggnog in your fridge,' said Ross, pulling on his coat. 'I'll come back tomorrow night and we'll have some more.'

Briana shook her head. 'Really, you don't have to. I'll manage.'

'Sure you will,' he mocked. 'Only two and a half thousand or so left.'

'It's my own stupid fault.'

'So? What's that got to do with it? We all make stupid mistakes. And what are friends for anyway?' He came closer and drew her into his arms. 'And don't tell me I can't kiss you, because I will anyway.'

She let it happen, standing in his arms without resisting, feeling like a fraud.

'I wish you wouldn't do that, Ross,' she said gently when he released her.

He looked down at her with a grin. 'What harm is there in an innocent kiss between friends? Besides, there's a full moon tonight. How could I possibly help myself?'

Briana laughed. 'You're incorrigible, Ross.'

He opened the door. 'Yeah, my mother used to say that. Good night, curlyhead. See you tomorrow.'

She fell into bed, more tired than she'd felt for a long time, and slept straight through the night.

Brand came into her workroom the next day. Her stomach tightened at the sight of him. She wasn't sure if it was nerves or anger. He surveyed the room, frowning, then the grey eyes searched for hers and she met them defiantly. He approached the table at which she was organising an assignment for Jim.

'Isn't anybody working on the Payne order?' he asked.

She nodded at Sally. 'Sally is.'

'They want it back by Tuesday!'

She gritted her teeth. 'They'll have it!' She turned her back and walked into her office. She wasn't going to argue with him in front of her workers. He followed her in and closed the door behind him.

'May I remind you that Thanksgiving weekend is coming up? Where are you going to find the time?'

'I'll find it!' Her heart was pounding hard. She couldn't stand him!

'Why don't you have more of your people working on it?'

'Because we have other work to do! We have another deadline next week. Just let me worry about it, all right?'

He looked at her silently for a moment. 'If you need help, let me know. I can find someone to help out on a temporary basis.'

She clenched her teeth. 'I don't need any help.'

It was stupid and childish to say that, but she couldn't help it. She wasn't going to ask him for help if she had to sit up nights doing the job herself.

He shrugged, turned and strode out.

She sat down at her desk, feeling the crazy desire to burst into tears.

True to his word, Ross came back again that evening to help her. He poured them each some eggnog again, his eyes laughing. 'I'll make a drinker out of you yet.'

'I wouldn't hold my breath if I were you.' She took the glass and smiled. 'Thanks. What would I do without you?'

'Sit here by yourself and do it,' he said drily. 'Come on, let's get going. Would you believe I *dreamed* about the damned things last night? Pins with little red dots were floating through the air and I had to catch them and I couldn't. They kept slipping through my fingers.' He made a tortured face. 'A real nightmare, I tell you.'

Briana laughed. 'Sounds like the type of dreams I have.'

'What did you dream about?'

'Nothing last night. I slept like a baby.'

He gave her a devilish wink. 'That was the eggnog. Very therapeutic sometimes.'

Despite the boring work, the evening was fun. They watched some silly comedies on TV, made sillier yet by Ross's humorous commentaries.

'When does this have to be ready?' he asked suddenly.

'They want it on Tuesday. I'll have to finish it by Monday night.'

Ross frowned. 'How are you going to get it done? All you have is tomorrow and Monday.'

'I'll get some extra help on Monday if I need it.' All she had to do was ask Brand, but she wouldn't need any help. She'd be home for the next few days and had plenty of time to finish the job herself. She hadn't told Ross she wasn't flying to Florida after all. There wasn't a doubt in her mind that he would insist on taking her home with him and she'd have no good reason to refuse.

'Thanks very much for all the help,' she said when he left. 'Have a nice Thanksgiving.'

'You too. I'll drop by on Monday and see if you've finished.'

She felt deflated after he'd left. The rest of the week stretched out in grey loneliness. Well, she'd have enough work to do to fill the time!

Wednesday night she sat again in front of the TV surrounded by little plastic bags. There was a good movie on and she watched while, with mechanical movements, she drew out pins, reversed them and stuck them back in. She'd keep on doing it until the end of the movie at eleven. Then she'd go to bed.

It was almost eleven when she heard a car stop in front of the house. A car door slammed. The wooden boards of the front porch creaked under heavy footsteps. Her heart jumped into her throat. Who could be here at this hour? The doorbell rang. She sat perfectly still, fear churning in her stomach. Again the bell rang, followed by a loud knocking.

'Briana!'

Her heart dropped back into her chest at the sound of the familiar voice. Brand! Relief flooded her. Not that she was particularly anxious to see him, but at least he wasn't a prowler. She got up and opened the door.

He looked very big standing there in the dark. His expression, as he looked at her, and past her into the room, did not inspire thoughts of peace and friendliness.

'What the hell is going on here?'

The tone of his voice antagonised her. She stood in the door, giving him no opportunity to pass. '*Nothing* is going on. And what are you doing here at this hour of the night? You scared the living daylights out of me!'

'I was passing by and I noticed the lights. You are supposed to be in Florida by now, remember? I thought some prowler was helping himself to your possessions. Then I noticed your car was still here. Are you going to let me in? I'm freezing my tail off.' He took a step forward and automatically she stepped back. Shrugging she closed the door.

His eyes swept the room, taking in the boxes, the little plastic bags, the blaring TV. She switched it off and stared at him in the sudden silence. The air crackled with tension. The grey eyes looked at her hard.

'Why are you still here? Did you miss your plane?'

'I didn't miss it. I cancelled it.'

'You *cancelled* it? Are you out of your mind?'

'No,' she said drily, looking at the mess on the floor, 'not yet. But I'm getting there.'

'What the hell do you think you're doing?'

'What does it look as if I'm doing? I'm pulling out little pins, turning them around and sticking them back in.'

He swore under his breath, closing his eyes for a fraction of a second as if asking for divine help. 'Is that why you cancelled your trip home?'

'No.' She gave a short, humourless laugh. 'I may be stupid, but I'm not crazy. My father had to go to Tokyo and my mother went with him.'

His eyes narrowed. 'So no Thanksgiving dinner.'

She shrugged, as if she didn't care. 'No. They did invite me to come along to Japan.' She didn't know why she said that.

'And you declined?'

'Of course I did. Payne before pleasure,' she mocked.

He glanced back at the boxes on the floor. 'I want

you to put this stuff away this minute, then go to bed and get some rest. Tomorrow morning at eight I'll pick you up and you can help me with that damned bird that's been filling up my refrigerator for the past three days.'

'No thank you,' she said politely. 'I have other plans.'

'Such as what?'

'It's none of your business!'

He gave a tortured sigh. 'Briana, will you stop this nonsense? What are you going to do? Sit here all day tomorrow fitting little pins into holes?'

'It has to be done, doesn't it? I made a stupid mistake and I intend to fix it.'

'I'll have someone in to help you on Monday. And we can pull one of the girls from the kitchen.'

She didn't answer, but went down on her knees to pick up the little plastic bags. She'd emptied the box on the floor so she could pick the bags up more easily.

'I'll give you a hand.' He stripped off his sheepskin jacket and tossed it on a chair. He sat on his haunches next to her, scooping up handfuls of the bags and tossing them into the box.

She was so tired. Her eyes ached from straining them too much and the sight of the piles of parts still to be fixed was hopelessly discouraging. She was uncomfortably aware of him so close next to her, this man who'd made her more angry than she'd been for a long time, who'd made her feel like a fool for making a stupid mistake. She swallowed with difficulty, her eyes watering. She wiped at them with the back of her hand.

Why was she trembling? She leaned one hand on the floor for support. She was cracking up; in a minute she would burst into tears. She wished he would go. She didn't want him here, making her feel even more miserable. Lowering her head, she tried desperately to control the trembling. Her throat ached.

'Briana?' His voice seemed unreal. 'Are you all right?'

She nodded fiercely, her throat unable to emit a sound, her body rigid.

'Oh, my God,' he said huskily, putting his arms around her and drawing her against him. Her face landed against his shoulder, the wool of his sweater soft against her cheek. His hand was warm on the back of her neck. Something broke inside her and her body slumped against him. She took a shuddering breath.

'Don't cry,' he whispered against her ear. 'I'm sorry. I'm sorry I was such a bastard. Don't cry, please . . .'

CHAPTER SEVEN

HE held her, stroking her hair as if she were a child. She took another deep breath, feeling the misery fade away. They sat very still for a long time, the silence filled with the sound of her heart drumming in her chest. She couldn't move. Her body lay against him in limp surrender.

Something was happening. In the shadowy depths of her consciousness there was a shivering of awareness, but thoughts could not clearly capture the meaning. There was only sensation now—the heady delight of his body against her, his fingers in her hair. This was another world, a world of soft, warm light and singing sensations.

Then he moved, adjusting her head as his mouth came down on hers in swift possession. He kissed her with hungry urgency, his arm pressing her against him in desperate need. Her lips parted and his tongue touched hers. A wave of heat washed over her and her senses reeled. She yielded to him, returning his kiss with a depth of emotion that staggered her with its intensity.

His hands began to wander over her body, sliding along her hips and moving up to her breasts. They responded to his touch instantly and almost painfully, and he suddenly dragged himself away, breathing hard. Flushed and light-headed, Briana fought to catch her breath. Raking his fingers through his hair, he sought her eyes and a hot wave of self-consciousness rushed through her. She lowered her gaze, seeing her hands tremble. The silence quivered between them, but she knew no words to break it. There was nothing to say, nothing to explain.

She turned away slowly, reaching for a handful of bags and dropping them in the box. Her hand was still trembling. He moved forward doing the same and in silence they finished clearing everything away.

Then there was nothing more to do. His eyes met hers and in the grey depths she read the unspoken question. Her mouth went dry and a deep, aching longing surfaced, yet she couldn't make herself say the words to make him stay.

He reached for his coat, slipping it on as he crossed the room to the door.

'I'll pick you up at eight in the morning,' he said quietly.

She nodded wordlessly.

'Good night, Briana.'

'Good night.'

He turned and strode into the night, down the path to his car. She watched him as he unlocked it and got in. The air was frigid and she shivered as she closed the door.

The bed felt cold and empty. She should have asked him to stay. He had wanted her; she'd wanted him, too, and he'd known that. Closing her eyes, she could still feel his mouth on hers, still taste his kiss, still feel his hand on her breast.

She dreamed of him that night. And in the dream he was kissing her and caressing her body as he slowly took off her clothes. They made beautiful love, full of exquisite passion. And then he got up and looked down at her with contempt in his eyes. 'You're lousy in bed, you know,' he said coldly, turning away to pull on his clothes.

She woke up sobbing, the sheets and blankets twisted around her, the pillow on the floor.

The insistent ringing of the doorbell penetrated her sleep and Briana dragged herself out of bed, getting her left leg caught in the sheet and almost falling on her face. Clutching at the bedside table for support, her eye caught the alarm clock. Five past eight! Through the fogginess of semi-consciousness she remembered. Brand was here to take her home to cook that blasted turkey for him. She felt a stirring of resentment. Oh, Lord, she wanted to sleep. Let him cook his own turkey.

Again the ringing shrilled through the air. In another minute he'd break down the door. Grabbing her robe off the chair she hastily made her way to the front door and opened it. Cold air rushed in and she shivered, stepping aside as Brand came in.

'Good morning,' he said cheerfully, giving her a quick appraising look. 'I knew I'd better come and get you or you'd never make it.' There was no accusation in his voice, only amusement and she felt her heart give a little lurch as she looked into his eyes. The dream came back to her and she felt a rush of warmth come into her face. For a long time afterwards she'd lain awake, falling asleep eventually from sheer exhaustion.

'I forgot to set my alarm last night. I was so tired I just dropped. I'll get ready now.' She turned and rushed out of the room, feeling like a fool. She must look a sight too, with her hair standing wildly out in all directions as it always did after she'd been asleep.

'Shall I make you some coffee?' he called after her, and she stopped with her hand on the bedroom door.

'If you don't mind. The coffee is in the cabinet to the left of the sink.'

'I'll fix you some breakfast at my place, okay?'

'Fine.'

She showered quickly, pulled on jeans and a sweater, brushed her hair out and made up her face. Later in the day she'd have to change into her good clothes. She'd just have to take them along. Frowning, she searched through her closet, picking out a soft wool dress of lavender blue and tossed it on to the unmade bed. Quickly she found tights, shoes, jewellery and put them all on the bed. There was a knock on the door.

'Are you decent?'

She groaned inwardly. Couldn't he have waited until she came out? The room was a mess—the bed unmade, her wet towel flung on the floor, clothes everywhere. 'Come in.'

He had a mug of coffee in his hand and she took it from him, feeling uneasy with him there in her bedroom. 'Thanks.'

'You're welcome. His eyes slid over her. 'You do work fast.'

Had he expected to find her still in a state of undress? She shrugged. 'I'm just wearing my kitchen uniform. I'll have to change later. It'll save time if I just bring my things now and do it at your house, if you don't mind.'

'Sure, I hadn't even thought of it.'

She wondered what other things he hadn't thought of. She hoped he had all the necessary ingredients to make stuffing for the turkey. Well, she'd do the best she could.

She took a sip from her coffe. It was good and strong, just what she needed. 'Good coffee,' she commented and he grinned.

'I'm not totally incompetent in the kitchen, if you can believe that.' He surveyed the room, making no motion to leave. 'Whose toys are those?' he asked, pointing at the old dolls on a shelf above the chest of drawers.

She swallowed a mouthful of coffee. 'My mother's. This used to be her room when she was a girl.' She wondered what he was thinking. Briana, the spoiled little rich girl, had a mother who'd grown up in this modest little house in the Virginia countryside. She began to fold her clothes and put them in a small overnight case, tossing in her make-up, perfume, comb and brush.

'I'm ready.' She found her purse and took the overnight case off the bed. She'd just have to leave the room the way it was. He followed her out into the living room, where he put on his coat. She found her own and slipped it on as they walked out the door.

'Why don't I take my own car?' she suggested. 'That way you won't have to take me back home tonight.'

'I know my manners. I'm picking you up and I'm taking you home.' And without further ado he steered her to his car and held the door open for her.

She'd never given much thought to the place where he lived, but when he stopped in front of his house, she was slightly taken aback. It was a lovely old house surrounded by a large garden with big old trees. It was made of wood and had a large porch wrapped around two sides. The green window shutters were open and a large chimney promised a fireplace inside. Was this *his* house? How could he possibly afford a place like this? Well, maybe it wasn't his. Maybe he just rented it.

'Are you coming?' His voice was amused as if he had guessed her thoughts.

'This is a wonderful old house,' she said, following him up the steps to the porch.

'You sound surprised,' he commented. 'Something strange about me having a wonderful old house?'

'I hadn't expected it, that's all.'

'What had you expected?' He gave her an enquiring look as he put the key in the lock and turned it.

She shrugged, feeling more awkward by the moment. What was she supposed to say? That she'd expected him to live in a rented apartment or in one of the new town houses? Somewhere small and convenient and more suitable for bachelorly living. 'I hadn't really thought about it.'

'I had an apartment until four years ago. Then I found myself in more prosperous circumstances and went looking for a house. I was lucky to get this.'

So he did own it. Had he inherited some money? She was dying to know, but good manners kept her from asking the question. It's a drag to be so well-brought-up, she thought wryly.

Brand opened the door and let her in. 'I haven't had much time to fix it up. It needs a lot of work. I bought it from an old man who'd lived here practically all his life. He moved to Richmond to live with his daughter.'

She loved the house at first sight—the heavy wooden doors, the high ceilings, the wide, sweeping staircase. The living room was comfortably furnished, but the rest of the place looked rather bare with no rugs on the wooden floors and only a few pieces of furniture.

'You'd better show me the kitchen. We'd need to get that turkey in the oven as soon as possible. What time are you planning to eat?'

'I told everyone to come at three. We can eat at four or so.'

The kitchen was old-fashioned and not very big, but it contained a decent stove and a built-in dishwasher, which was a relief. If there was anything she hated, it was doing dishes after a big party. Not that she'd be obliged to do them, but she would anyway, probably.

'Let's have a look at the bird,' she suggested as he opened the refrigerator.

'First I'll fix you some breakfast. And I'll make us some more coffee.'

She peeked past his arm as he took out the eggs. The turkey took up half of the top shelf and dominated the interior. 'How big is it?' she asked.

'Almost fourteen pounds. How long will it need to cook?'

'I don't remember exactly. Twelve, fifteen minutes per pound probably. It should say on the wrapping. You have a cook book?'

'*Fanny Farmer's*, over there.' He pointed to the counter and she picked up the big, brand-new book.

'Did you buy this for the occasion?'

He grinned. 'No, it was a present from a friend not long ago. She said it was very good and very basic and any idiot could cook from it.'

'Well then, why do you need me?' she asked lightly.

'Moral support. I'm a blundering beginner and turkeys terrify me. How about a cheese omelette?'

'Sounds terrific.' Why was she nervous? Calm down, she told herself.

'Don't just stand there, sit,' he ordered, motioning to a chair. She sat, her stomach hollow with nerves. Or was it hunger? She watched with interest as he worked. The bulk of him seemed rather out of place in the small kitchen, but he moved with ease and familiarity and offered her a plate of food in an amazingly short time.

He sat with her while she ate, drinking a cup of coffee, telling her about the things he wanted to do to the house when he found the time.

'So when are you going to find time?' she asked. 'You're always working. Is it really necessary?'

He shrugged. 'No, probably not, but I'm so used to working all the time, I wouldn't know what to do with myself if I weren't.'

'They have a word for that,' she commented, biting into a piece of toast. 'And what you could do is fix up your house.'

He grinned. 'I can't fight logic like that. More coffee?'

It was an unexpectedly companionable time, the talk easy and flowing naturally. Her eggs finished, she pushed the plate away.

'Thanks, that was good. Now show me what you have in mind for the stuffing.'

He frowned. 'Well, I wasn't sure. There's a whole list of different recipes and I didn't know which one would be best. I haven't any idea what all those herbs are supposed to taste like.' He made a helpless gesture, grinning. 'I did buy a batch of them and some bags of croûtons.'

It was interesting to see him so unsure of himself. The kitchen was not his natural habitat, that was obvious. The shop was where he really belonged. There he was lord and master, told everybody what to do, and knew all the answers to all the questions.

'I have a recipe of my own that's very good,' she offered. 'It has raisins and walnuts in it. You have all those?'

'I do.' He turned and went in search of the requested items. He placed them on the work-surface and looked at her questioningly. 'What else?'

'You have port?'

He frowned. 'Port as in wine?'

'Yes. It's good in the stuffing. I may not drink it, but I like to cook with it. If you don't have it, sherry will do.'

'I have both.' He went out to get it and Briana looked around to find what she needed. It had been a long time since she'd cooked for a large gathering. Cliff had loved having elaborate parties and she had enjoyed cooking and baking. They could have easily had the affairs catered, but she'd never wanted to. There was plenty of time for planning and organising and shopping and getting the apartment ready. It gave her something to do. The apartment kitchen was large and well-equipped with the latest appliances and it was a joy to work in.

Her life had been perfect, or so she'd thought. She'd loved Cliff, had been obsessed by him—his charm, his good looks, his happy-go-lucky personality. She'd loved the nights, the mornings when they woke up together in the king-sized bed, their bodies warm with sleep, eager for each other again . . .

But there had been signs, and she'd ignored them subconsciously. She hadn't wanted to know that her paradise was not perfect and that her prince had some fatal flaws.

'Here you go.' Brand put a bottle in front of her. 'What were you dreaming about? You looked a thousand miles away.'

She shook her head as if to clear her thoughts, feeling treacherous colour creep into her face. 'Nothing.' She picked up the bottle and pretended to read the label, avoiding his eyes.

'Is that all right?'

'Sure, fine.' She put the wine down. 'I need a big bowl.'

They worked together for some time—Briana mixing and cooking, Brand fetching and carrying. By eleven the turkey was stuffed and trussed and ready for the oven and the kitchen resembled a disaster area. Briana glanced around and grimaced apologetically. 'I didn't say I was a neat worker. I must have used every dish and utensil you own.'

'They'll wash.' He was smiling into her eyes and she felt suddenly warm and uneasy. Averting her eyes, she picked up a dish at random and carried it to the sink. Good Lord, what was the matter with her?

He stood behind her and with his hands on her shoulders gently turned her to face him. His eyes held hers for several endless moments and she couldn't drag her gaze away.

'Thanks for coming,' he said quietly.

'It's nothing. I . . . I . . . my hands are wet. I'm dripping all over everything,' she babbled. 'I need a towel . . .'

Leaning slightly to the left he reached for the towel, his eyes not leaving her face. He took one of her hands, dried it as if she were a helpless child, massaging it gently between the soft cloth. She didn't move, submitting to his ministrations with a peculiar sense of fascination. It was an oddly sensual feeling to have him take each finger and dry it as if it were a delicate piece of china.

'What are you doing?' she whispered, as if there were anyone else in the room who might overhear.

'I'm drying your hands,' he whispered back, his eyes sparking laughter. He lowered the hand he was holding and took the other one, repeating the procedure at his leisure. When he was finished, he flung the towel on to a chair and lifted her hand to examine it.

'Beautiful hand,' he commented. He turned it over, and ran a finger gently over her palm. She tried to pull it away, but he took a firm grip on it and she stood helplessly caught while he went on stroking her palm, looking into her eyes with an amused half-smile. Then he bent his head and touched his lips to her hand. She felt a curling sensation in her stomach, then the moist heat of the tip of his tongue as it trailed along her palm. A little gasp escaped her and she wrenched at her hand, but he held it tightly. He straightened, lowering her hand and sliding his hands up her arms to her neck, moving under her hair, cradling her head.

'Now you have nice dry hands,' he said as if speaking to a child. 'Is that better?'

'Much.' Her voice was faint. She stared at his mouth, only inches away, feeling the frantic beating of her heart, the warm rush of longing. She began to tremble and she closed her eyes, feeling at the same time the warm, gentle touch of his mouth on hers. He teased her with his lips, brushing them sensuously across hers, slowly, softly, tantalising her senses. Her arms, hanging limp by her sides, moved up around his back, broad and muscular under her fingers. Her lips parted and his explorations intensified, making the blood pound in her head. His arms slid down and pulled her closer against him. The hard, muscled tenseness of his body pressed intimately against her own and she felt suddenly dizzy with longing for more. His obvious arousal and her own helpless desire sparked in her a sudden panic. She gasped for breath, struggling to free herself.

'Don't,' she muttered huskily, taking a trembling step backwards, avoiding his gaze.

'What's the matter?' His tone was urgent, surprised. He lifted her chin, forcing her to look at him. She twisted her face free of his grasp.

'Nothing's the matter. I just think we'd better stop this.'

'Why? I thought you were rather enjoying it.'

'That's not the point.'

'I'm glad you're not denying it.' He drew her to him again, kissing her with passionate determination and holding her very tightly so she couldn't move. She fought him for a moment, then strength seemed to drain from her. Whispering, wordless thoughts filled her mind. No form, no shape, no substance to the sensations. No reality but quivering emotions. She was trembling when he released her. His eyes looked into hers, holding her gaze. The silence was alive with vibrant emotion. His hand came up and softly stroked her cheek.

'Last night,' he said softly, 'I wanted more than anything to stay with you.'

'I know,' she whispered, staring at his broad chest, aching to be in his arms again, feel his heart beat under her hands. 'But I don't want an affair with you.' She turned towards the sink and gripped the edge.

'Don't you trust me?'

'I don't trust anybody.' She turned on the tap, too far, too fast. Water splashed into a bowl and back up against her shirt, her face. 'Oh, damn,' she muttered.

He handed her the towel. She avoided his eyes, rubbing her midriff furiously with the towel. She didn't want to feel this way about him, to have these helpless, obsessive feelings. It could lead to nothing but disaster. She didn't like him. She didn't trust him. She tossed the towel over the back of a chair, searching for something to say to change the subject. 'How are you planning to seat everyone? Your table won't take twelve.'

For a moment he did not answer, his silence clearly intentional. 'I borrowed a couple of card tables,' he said then. 'We can put one on either end.'

She nodded. 'Tablecloths?'

'My mother loaned me a couple, but I'm not sure how they fit.'

'We'd better try them out then.'

'You're so clever,' he said some time later, looking at the now-long table with the two white tablecloths spread out over it and a smaller square one diagonally across the middle to hide the overlapping edges. The small one was green and white and looked appropriate for the occasion. He'd borrowed it from his neighbour lady, who'd been rather amazed to find Brand at her door asking for a tablecloth.

'She wondered if I needed help,' he said, grinning. 'She didn't seem to have much confidence in me, either.'

'I hope your friends have enough confidence in you to show up today, or we're going to have a lot of turkey and stuffing for the two of us.' She surveyed the table with a critical eye.

'We need a centrepiece,' she decided, warming to the preparation. 'Bet you didn't think about that?'

He shook his head. 'I thought about the tables and the turkey. I hoped the details would fall into place or quietly go away.'

She laughed. 'Details never go quietly away. If you ignore them they grow into unmanageable monsters that make your life miserable. You, of all people, should know that.'

'When it comes to a turkey dinner I thought I could probably manage the monster,' he answered drily. 'And the lack of a centrepiece probably won't spoil anyone's appetite.'

'True. But we'll come up with something.'

Which she did. An arrangement of nuts, fresh cranberries and shiny apples on a shallow dish with evergreen branches clipped from one of the trees outside. Some small acorns and pinecones completed the arrangement.

'Very artistic,' he commented, standing back from the table to survey her handiwork. 'Have you done this sort of thing before?'

'Plenty of times.'

'When you were married?'

'Yes.' She looked away. 'Do you have candles?'

'Forget the candles. Let's talk about you.'

'I don't want to talk about me.'

'I want to know about you, Briana.' The quiet, determined tone of his voice made her look up. She met his eyes, and the intense regard in the grey depths made her uneasy. He smiled ruefully.

'You really don't trust me very much, do you?'

She shook her head. 'No. And you don't trust me, either.'

'I didn't. Past tense. You proved yourself.' He paused. 'I suppose I haven't yet.' His tone was wry. 'Well, let me see if I can find some candles.'

Briana had no idea what kind of people would be friends of Brand's, but she was surprised to find them a casual, relaxed group of people from various walks of life, most of them married or otherwise attached. She was aware of the speculation in their eyes as Brand introduced her, but found no antagonism or jealousy lurking in any.

Among his friends, Brand was like a different person. He was more relaxed than she'd ever seen him before. Both men and women talked and joked with him with the ease of long familiarity and Briana couldn't help compare this with the fearful politeness of Kathleen and Margaret at the workshop office. The contradictions in his character fascinated her. Who was this man? What other facets of his personality were there yet to be discovered? She kept herself in the background, listening and observing, doing little of the talking. Now and then she went back into the kitchen to check on the turkey and to deal with other preparations for the meal.

Someone offered her a glass of eggnog from a tray and after a moment's hesitation she accepted. Brand came to find her moments later. 'Are you hiding?' he asked. 'I keep looking for you and you're in the kitchen or in some corner like a timid Cinderella. Are you all right? You don't have to take care of everything yourself, you know. You're not hired help. This is a co-operative effort.'

'I'm fine. I'm enjoying myself, really.'

He frowned. 'Are you uncomfortable with all these strangers?'

She laughed, shaking her head. One thing she had learned in her life was how to move among strangers. 'Mixing and mingling is one of my talents,' she said lightly. 'Only today I feel more like listening and observing.' She was enjoying discovering this new man, hearing from his friends things she'd probably never hear from Brand himself. She'd already found out, among other things, that the generous benefactor of the group home was no one less than Brand himself.

He gave her a quizzical look. 'Listening and observing? You make this sound like some performance, some show.'

She laughed. 'Oh, but it is! You have some very amusing friends. Did you hear that one over there—Bob, I think his name is—the surgeon? He was describing a gall bladder operation in minute detail and he managed to make it sound like a Broadway comedy. Remind me not to ask for him if I need my gall bladder out.'

Brand laughed. 'Actually, he's one of the best, although one part of his poor soul yearns to be a comedian. Of course, aspiring to be a comedian is not considered a serious avocation, so he decided to be a surgeon instead. Don't ask me why. And what the hell are you drinking?' His expression had changed dramatically as if the discovery of the glass of eggnog in her hand had come as a great shock.

'Eggnog.'

'It's loaded with liquor!'

'I can tell,' she said drily.

'You told me you don't drink! What do you think you're doing?'

His concern was touching and rather surprising at that. She laughed. 'Don't look so shocked. I'm only having this one glass and I'm sipping it. It'll take me an hour before I finish it. I promise you I won't get drunk.'

'I thought you didn't like liquor, now I see you drinking this. Of course I'm shocked.'

'How much have you had yourself? You seem rather emotional about the whole thing.'

'Emotional? Me, emotional? I'm never emotional. I'm just rather concerned about the fact that you're resorting to drink at my party. Being here among all these strangers, you probably feel left out and unsure of yourself and I never even thought about it. And here you are drinking, to give yourself courage, you who are not used to drinking, and . . .'

'Brand! Will you stop it? What's the matter with you? Are you drunk?' She couldn't believe what she was hearing. She'd never heard him carry on this way. 'How much of this stuff have you had? Some host you are! Let me make you some coffee, before . . .' It was then that she saw the devilish gleam in his eyes and a moment later he'd pulled her to his side, laughing out loud.

'Oh, my, how gullible you are!'

She felt like a total fool and was at a loss for words. How could she have been so easily fooled? 'I'd better check on the turkey,' she said, gathering the remnants of her dignity. 'I think it should be about done.'

Half an hour later they were all seated around the table and Brand raised his glass, looking around the table, his eyes reaching Briana's and stopping there.

'As you all can tell from the looks of this beautiful table and the luscious turkey sitting in front of me,' he began in his deep, resonant voice, sounding like a preacher, 'I've had some help, some considerable help I should say. It has saved all of us from the culinary disaster I would have undoubtedly presented you with in my well-meaning, but bungling way. I do want to thank all of you for coming, even though you must have been expecting the worst. It was an act of courage and proof of great friendship.'

'Hear, hear,' somebody said, and Brand glared at him.

'So,' he continued, 'this is a toast for Briana, the leading lady of the turkey drama.'

Briana smiled her most modest smile, clinking her glass of Perrier with the others containing wine.

The meal was a great success. The various dishes brought in by the guests were arranged on the table, a feast of many colours—the orange of candied yams, the green of a leafy salad, the ruby red of a cranberry relish. The turkey was cooked to perfection and the stuffing was raved over by all. Across the table Briana was aware of Brand's eyes resting on her from time to time. It made her uncomfortable and she tried to avoid his gaze, which was not easy.

Dinner was a long, drawn-out affair with light-hearted talk and a lot of laughter. No one was in a hurry and the food disappeared slowly from the bowls and platters as the guests kept taking further helpings.

Brand was making her feel increasingly uneasy with the way he was looking at her and she was glad when the meal was finally over and she could keep herself busy clearing the table, stacking dishes into the dishwasher and generally cleaning up. There was plenty of help from the others. Briana listened to the disjointed snatches of conversation coming from the people moving in and out of the kitchen, most of which did not make any sense to her at all. One woman, Ella, a sultry-looking brunette with bedroom eyes, displayed great interest in Brand's house, explaining her ideas of how he should furnish the various rooms. Apparently she had given it quite some thought as her suggestions went into considerable detail.

'I'd like to him do *something* about this place,' she said in general, looking around the kitchen to see if she had any takers on the idea. 'It looks as empty as it did last year. If he doesn't have the time, he could get a decorator to do it for him. He's got the money for it. Just think of what it could look like! It's such a beautiful place and he doesn't do a thing with it. What a waste!' At which moment Brand entered the kitchen. 'I was just talking about you,' she said, undaunted by his appearance. 'Why don't you do something about this house? You might as well have an apartment the way you live in it.'

'I'm going to,' he said levelly.

'When?' she persisted.

'Soon.'

'What is soon? You said that last year.'

'Don't be difficult, Ella. You sound like a nagging wife.'

'That's what you need. A wife.'

'Are you applying?' he asked.

She flashed him a dazzling smile. 'Not in a million years, dear Brand. I've known you too long and you make lousy husband material.'

'Thanks a lot,' he said drily. 'Hand me the coffee, will you? In the cabinet behind that insulting little head of yours.'

Ella gave him the coffee can, grinned and kissed him

on the cheek. 'Don't be disappointed. You'll find someone else.' With which she swept out of the kitchen.

Briana was amazed to see Brand the recipient of such casual, familiar treatment. If she'd ever tell Kathleen and Margaret, which she wouldn't, they'd never believe it in a hundred years. Her eyes met Brand's.

'You have liptstick on your cheek,' she said.

He offered her his other cheek. 'Why don't you put some on the other side, then I'll be symmetrical.'

She laughed. 'Sorry, no lipstick. It got eaten with the turkey.' She handed him a paper towel and he began to rub his cheek.

'Why don't you have Ella do your house?' she asked. 'She has it all figured out. She told us in detail.'

'I want to do it myself,' he said. 'Besides, I'm not sure I'd survive the experience. I love her dearly for short periods far between.' He proceeded to put coffee and water into an enormous electric perculator, plugged it in and left it to perk.

Briana wondered if he'd once loved Ella dearly for prolonged periods closer together, but for some reason doubted it. A small blonde with the theatrical name of Esmeralda entered the kitchen and began to cut up two large pumpkin pies and put the wedges on dessert plates on a tray.

'Do you know where the mixer is?' she asked Briana. 'I brought some cream, but I didn't whip it yet.'

Briana opened one of the cabinets and took the mixer out. 'There's a bowl on the shelf over there,' she said, motioning with her head. One morning in Brand's kitchen fixing food, and she knew where everything was.

'You really did a fantastic job on that turkey,' Esmeralda said, pouring cream from the carton into the bowl. 'I'm glad you were here to help Brand.' She grinned. 'To tell you the truth, I had my doubts about Brand cooking today, *Fanny Farmer*, or no *Fanny Farmer.*'

'You gave it to him?'

She nodded. 'It started out as a joke, actually, which is a long and convoluted story you don't want to hear. Let's just say cooking is not Brand's forté. His talents lie in different directions.' She stared into the bowl of cream, the mixer in her hand, ready to whip. Then she lifted her face and clear blue eyes looked right at Briana. 'I hope you'll be good to him,' she said quietly.

The words took Briana by surprise and she stared at Esmeralda without answering.

'He deserves some happiness for himself,' Esmeralda went on. 'He's always thinking of others, always working. I don't know how he does it.' She paused, still looking at Briana, waiting for some sort of acknowledgment.

Briana nodded. 'I know what you mean.' She felt uneasy.

'I think that's what went wrong with Christa. I don't think she really understood him, but he should have given her more of his time. In a way it was surprising she stayed around as long as she did.' Esmeralda stared into the bowl, frowning, as if puzzled by the logic of her own reasoning. 'I guess what he needs is somebody who's tough enough to let him be what he needs to be without taking a back seat, if that makes any sense.' She looked up, meeting Briana's eyes. Then she grimaced, smiling. 'Oh, listen to me, playing analyst again. I'm sure you can take care of yourself and you look perfectly capable of taking on Brand without my help.'

Briana shook her head, giving a half smile. 'Our relationship is not what you think it is, Esmeralda.'

Esmeralda gave her a searching look. 'I saw the way he looked at you at the dinner table.'

Briana was well aware of the way he had looked at her. She began scooping sugar into the sugar bowl, not answering.

'I'm sorry,' said Esmeralda. 'It's none of my business. Forget I said anything. She turned on the mixer and the whirring sound filled the kitchen, effectively cutting off the conversation.

It was well past midnight before everyone had left. Everything was picked up and cleared away. They'd run the dishwasher twice and Briana had half-filled it again with the last coffee cups and wine glasses.

'I think it's time I went,' she said casually. 'Would you mind taking me home now?' She wished she'd insisted on coming in her own car. It would have made it easier to leave.

'Why don't you stay for a while? Come, sit here with me in front of the fire.'

'Please, I'd rather go now, Brand.'

He gave her a long, searching look. 'Why are you afraid of me?' he asked at last.

'I'm not.' She didn't like the way he looked at her, as if trying to probe the depths of her soul.

He shook his head in dismay. 'You seem so different suddenly. You're nervous. You were all easy self-confidence when I first met you in my office. What's happening here?'

'Nothing's happening. I just want to go home. It's late. I'm tired, and I have work to do tomorrow.'

It was the wrong thing to say. His face grew hard and his mouth twisted in anger. 'If you mean the Payne order, leave the damned things alone! It's a day off tomorrow. I don't want you to work. Is that clear?'

Her body tensed. 'I'll do with my free day what I want,' she said coldly.

He sighed, closing his eyes briefly. 'Here we go again.' He put his hands on her arms. 'Don't you see,

Briana? I want to be with you. I want to know more about you. I want to know you.'

'Why?'

'Why? I'll show you why.'

'No!' She drew away, but he was too fast for her. He drew her to him and his mouth found hers, kissing her hungrily, impatiently. She tensed with impotent anger; standing rigidly in his arms, fighting her emotions. She didn't want to give in, but the passion in his kiss, the feeling of him so close to her, drew all resistance from her. He drew away slightly, looking into her eyes. 'This is why,' he said huskily. 'Because I want you. Because I want to hold you and make love to you.' His hands moved gently down her sides, rested lightly on her hips, then slowly moved upward to her breasts, all the while looking into her eyes. She stood immobilised, not able to look away.

'For the past four months,' he continued, speaking in a slow, low voice, 'all I did was look at you. I watched you work, move your body, saw that shuttered look in those green eyes of yours. And I wanted to know what hid behind that look. I wanted to touch you and hold you and make love to you.' His hands caressed her breasts and suddenly she began to tremble violently and feeling rushed back into her. She pushed his hands away, taking a shaky breath.

'I don't want this,' she said, and her voice shook. 'I don't want to make love.'

CHAPTER EIGHT

IT was a lie. She wanted him to go on touching her, kissing her with that passionate urgency she'd felt in him. She wanted him to take her clothes off and make love to her. She wanted to feel the warmth of his body in bed with her, to know that he wanted her and loved her. Yet the courage to make herself vulnerable again failed her. 'I don't want to make love,' she repeated. But her voice lacked conviction and she could hear it herself.

'That's not true, Briana,' he said quietly. He didn't attempt to touch her now, but he was still too close for comfort.

She closed her eyes briefly. 'I'm not ready for a relationship. I made a mistake once, I'm not about to make another one. I want you to leave me alone.'

'He really did a job on you, didn't he?'

'And I learned my lesson. Now please take me home.'

'Will you stay and talk to me if I promise not to touch you?'

'I want to go home,' she said unsteadily.

'Please?'

She clenched her hands by her sides. 'There's nothing to talk about! I don't know what you want from me!'

'I just want to talk, to get to know more about you.' He paused. 'And I promise, boy scout's honour, hands off.'

He looked so humble and sincere, she almost smiled. She gave a light shrug. 'All right.'

'Sit here.' He pushed her gently down into a chair near the fire. Despite the heat from the brightly burning logs, she felt suddenly cold and empty inside and she shivered.

'Can I get you something hot? Coffee, tea?'

She nodded. 'Tea would be nice.'

He left the room and she huddled in the chair, pulling her legs under her and stared in the fire, seeing nothing. For some time she'd thought she'd never love another man and she hadn't cared. There had been a strange sort of comfort in the idea of living alone, of not needing anyone. There had been several men, back in Florida, who'd tried to break through her isolation without success. She hadn't been interested.

Something had changed these past few months. She'd felt lonely and she'd felt the stirring of longing for a man to share her life. And here was Brand, evoking in her all those long-buried feelings and sensations, making her feel alive again. He wanted her. She wanted him. But how long would it last? How long before he decided he wanted a change? No, she wasn't prepared to take the risk.

'Here you go. Do you take sugar or milk?'

She started, looking up in surprise. She had not heard him come in. He gave her an odd look as he placed a tray on a low table next to her chair.

'Just a little sugar.'

'There's some pumpkin pie left. Would you like a piece?'

She shook her head. 'I can't eat another thing for at least a week.'

'That's what I thought.' He handed her a glass mug and she stirred it absently, then put the spoon back on the tray.

'Do you have any brothers and sisters?' he asked and she looked at him in surprise.

He grinned. 'I have to start somewhere. This seemed like a pretty innocuous question.'

She gazed into her mug. 'I have no brothers and

sisters besides Tommy, and he died when he was twelve.'

'I remember.' He took a mouthful of tea. 'I have two sisters, Tammy, and Celia. Celia's a paediatrician. She's married and has two boys. They live in New Mexico.'

'Someone today mentioned that your father is a hot-shot corporate lawyer.' From the talk of his friends she'd understood that Brand's background was hardly one of poverty and deprivation. During most of his childhood they'd lived in a prestigious neighbourhood of Wáshington and when the two elder children had left for college his parents had bought a house in Leesburg and moved to an easier pace of life.

The corners of his mouth turned in a crooked smile. 'That sounds like an accusation. What's wrong with my father being a corporate lawyer?'

'Nothing.' She sounded defensive. 'Except that you treated me as if there was something wrong with having a moneyed background. You didn't like me because I was supposed to be a spoiled little rich girl. Well, you didn't exactly grow up poor yourself.'

'True, and I've known a lot of spoiled little rich girls. One thing I knew for sure, I wasn't having one in my workshop.'

'One look at me and you'd labelled me and tossed me on the heap, so to speak.'

'I believe I already apologised for that,' he said drily. 'So how come you didn't grow up spoiled rotten? Why are you now living in that little old house with all that godawful decrepit furniture as if you don't have a cent in the world?'

She stared at him for a moment, not answering. So that's how he saw it. 'It was my grandmother's house,' she said quietly. 'I like it there.'

'But it's not yours. Not the way it is.'

'And why not?'

'You're not an eighty-year-old country woman who

never had any money. I bet your own place in Florida didn't look one bit like it.' He gave her a questioning look and she shrugged.

He leaned forward, forearms resting on his thighs. 'Tell me, what did your place look like? Did you live in a house? An apartment?'

'An apartment. And you wouldn't have liked it. Why do you want to know?'

'The way people furnish and decorate their houses tells a lot about them.'

'Well, I didn't do mine. My husband had it done by some high-class decorator. A lot of chrome and glass and marble. And everything white and black. Would you believe we had white ceramic floor tiles all through the place, except the bedrooms?'

'Interesting.' He seemed amused. 'You didn't like it?'

'No. Oh, it was all very tasteful, you know, very expensive, but it didn't have any warmth, any real personality. It was like some public showroom.'

'So why didn't you do something about it?'

She gave a short, humourless laugh. 'Are you kidding? And spoil the effect?' She sighed. 'Actually, I tried once. I bought an oil painting, contemporary, very bright and colourful. It was a good piece and I really liked it. I hung it over the couch, which was white leather, and the whole room came alive. It was such a relief to see some colour in the place, I couldn't wait to show Cliff . . . my husband. I was convinced if he'd just see it, he'd like it.' She looked down at her tea mug, remembering.

'But he didn't,' Brand stated drily.

Briana looked up and grimaced. 'No. He said it spoiled the effect. So off came the painting and back up went the thing that I'd taken down.'

'What was that?'

'Take a wild guess. A charcoal drawing. Cliff wondered why I didn't like it. It had cost a fortune.

Actually, it was a beautiful picture.' She made a helpless gesture. 'That was the problem, you see, all the separate things were very nice. I couldn't object to them individually, I just wanted some colour in the place.' She pulled her mouth down in a rueful little smile. 'So I would buy flowers. Red tulips, orange chrysanthemums, or whatever I could find that had bright colours. I'd put them on the coffee table in the middle of the room, or on the dining room table. He never said anything about it, but I knew he didn't like it. Sometimes he'd buy me flowers. White roses, white carnations. Always white.' She shrugged. 'I decided not to fight it. It wasn't important, really.'

'Didn't you ever have a place of your own?' He was leaning back in his chair, long legs stretched out, eyeing her intently.

'I shared a walk-up apartment with a friend when I was in college. It was a small place and we just had cheap stuff, but it was cosy and we liked it. I got married right after I graduated.' She looked at her empty cup. 'I think I'd better go home now.'

'Where did you meet your husband?'

'Sailing.' She stood up, looking right at him. 'That's how he met all his women,' she added bitterly.

'He didn't marry them all.'

'No, he married me. Lucky me.' The sarcasm was hard to control.

'Why? Why did he marry you?'

She swallowed hard. 'Because he *loved* me. That's what he said.'

'And he didn't?'

'I thought he did,' she said tonelessly. 'Now, please, take me home. I really don't want to talk about this.'

After the incident she'd often wondered about it. Why *had* Cliff married her? Not because she was beautiful. Beautiful girls were a dime a dozen. Not because her father was rich. Cliff had money of his own, some of which was now hers as his widow. He had told her he loved her, but it had not lasted beyond the first year. One faithful, loving woman could not satisfy either his ego or his sexual appetite. He needed variety, the challenge of the chase, the excitement of yet another conquest.

Brand stood up without further delay and found her coat and case. They drove the short distance to her house, making light hearted conversation. He walked her out to the front door and wished her good night without any attempt to kiss her.

The doorbell rang at eleven the next morning. For a couple of hours now she'd been working on the Payne order, watching game shows on TV. She opened the door, finding a delivery man with an enormous flower arrangement.

'Briana Calloway?' he asked.

She nodded, taking the flowers from him in delighted surprise. 'Thank you.'

The bouquet was a riot of bright, beautiful colour—flowers of every kind and hue in a bold arrangement. A card was tucked between the greenery. *Some colour for your house,* she read. *With warm appreciation for your help yesterday. Brand.*

She placed the flowers on the coffee table in the living room, smiling at the beauty of the rainbow colours, smiling to herself.

She kept looking at the flowers as she worked. It was hard not to. The sheer size of the arrangement dominated the room. It was such an outrageous gesture, this enormous bouquet when something modest would have been quite adequate. Brand. So many sides to him. Rainbow colours from a rainbow man. The thought pleased her and for a moment she played with it in her mind, smiling to herself.

It was with some surprise that she found Brand at her door an hour later. Aware of the fluttering in her stomach, she let him in, quickly closing the door against the cold. He was wearing his sheepskin coat, but his head was bare and his hair looked as if the wind had been having fun with it. His eyes swept the room, noticing the flowers, the boxes and little bags of the Payne order on the floor.

'I knew you'd be working,' he said with resignation. 'There's no telling you, is there? Pigheaded as anybody I ever knew.'

'That's what they say about you. I suppose it takes one to know one. What were you doing this morning?' She held up her hand to stop him. 'No, let me guess. You were at the office.'

'We weren't talking about me. I'm the boss, remember? I can darn well do as I please. And I told you, no *ordered* you, not to work today.'

'You might as well get used to the fact that I don't take orders very well.' She smiled at him sweetly. 'I was just about to get myself some lunch. Would you care to join me, or did you eat already?'

He ran his hands through his dishevelled hair. 'No, I didn't. I actually hoped you'd feed me as long as it isn't cold turkey—I had that for breakfast.'

'Turkey, for *breakfast*?'

'Perfectly good food. Why ham, bacon, eggs, sausages, but not turkey? I opened the fridge this morning and it was sitting there, staring me in the face, begging me to take it out of its misery and get it over with. May I please take off my coat?'

'If you insist. The coat cupboard is next to the bathroom in the hall.'

'When he returned he had combed his hair. He rubbed his hands. 'This is more like January than November.' He sat down at the kitchen table, eyeing her appreciatively. 'I could get used to having you in the kitchen fixing food for me to eat, which I suppose is a terribly sexist thing to say, but please don't bite my head off.'

'Chicken noodle or cream of tomato?' she asked, ignoring his remarks.

'Tomato. Chicken is too much like turkey.' He stood up. 'Here, let me do that. I'm good at canned soup, expert actually.'

He took the can from her, taking not only the can, but her hand as well. Her heart began to beat erratically. They were very close, both clutching the can of soup, looking into each other's eyes. They stayed like that, silent, for a long suspended moment, the tension mounting.

She didn't resist as she knew she should. She didn't pull pack. She just stood there with a hollow ache of longing in her stomach. She could smell the warm male scent of him and his hand covering hers seemed to send out small electric currents thrilling through her body. She wanted him to kiss her, feel the gentle firmness of his lips against her own. She wanted his arms around her, to be held securely against that big, warm body. But what would happen if she gave in? She swallowed, dropping her gaze to his chest, to the thick wool sweater covering it. Her heart was beating a nervous rhythm and it seemed hard to breathe. She knew she had to say something, anything to break that silence and the shivering tension between them.

'Don't do this to me, Brand,' she whispered. 'Let me go. Please let me go.'

'I'm not letting you go, Briana.'

'Brand . . .'

He did not let her finish. The firmness of his lips on her trembling mouth silenced her. Gently he pried the soup can loose from her nerveless fingers and with his mouth still covering hers, he deposited it on the counter.

His arms moved around her, his hands slipping under her sweater and sliding up her bare back. Her lips parted under the pressure of his and her arms came up around his neck wanting to hold him, to be as close to him as possible.

'Briana,' he whispered, 'I love you.'

The words stilled every movement in her. 'What?' she said huskily, as if she hadn't heard. He withdrew slightly, looking at her in a way he'd never done before. His eyes had a strange smoky grey colour, an intensity of expression that confused her.

'I love you,' he repeated.

She shook her head. 'No, Brand, no.'

'Yes, Briana, yes,' he said softly. And for endless minutes he held her gaze, as if he could convince her with his eyes. And it was all there—warmth and love and concern and passion.

'Briana? Do you love me?' he asked at last.

Her throat went dry. 'I don't know. Love is a big word.'

'Yes. What do you feel for me, Briana?'

'I'm not sure. Mixed feelings, I suppose.' She tried to move out of his embrace, but he kept holding on. 'Please,' she pleaded, 'I need a little space. This is not very easy. I have to think. And I can't think very well when I'm too close to you.'

He released her, giving a lopsided grin. 'Well, that's encouraging. So tell me, what mixed feelings do you have?'

She ran the tip of her tongue along her dry lips. 'Parts of you I like. Other parts I don't. Yesterday, I watched you. I mean, I saw how you were with your friends, with me. You seemed relaxed, at ease and you were having a good time. You were actually quite human.'

'I told you, it happens sometimes.'

'Well, I had to experience it for myself. But it's confusing.' Absently, she picked up the can of soup, staring at the label, trying hard to focus her thoughts. 'You keep changing on me. You can be so cold and distant—I don't like that. I really couldn't stand you the first few times I met you, and that's putting it mildly. You were so damned arrogant and prejudiced and so opinionated and . . .'

'I remember you telling me that before.' He leaned lazily against the counter, hands in his pockets.

She took a deep breath. 'And then when the Payne order came back ... you didn't have to treat me like that. I know I made a mistake, but I can't be the first one ever to have made a mistake.'

'You weren't, actually. Julie once pulled a real zinger, and to be totally honest, which is not easy for me, I have been known to foul up once or twice myself.' He grinned quite disarmingly.

She looked back down on the can. 'Well, I don't know how to deal with those two different parts of your personality. It's as if you put on some kind of guise when you're at work, or deal with anything related to the shop. You become the big boss and everybody shivers in their shoes.'

'You don't exactly shiver,' he said mildly. 'You don't seem to have too much trouble dealing with me. You can hold your own quite well.'

'Well, I'm getting used to dealing with the unpleasant you. I'm not really used to you in your friendly mode.'

He straightened away from the counter. 'Well, I'd better show you more of my better side, I suppose, but being who I am I'm not sure how easy that is. To begin with I'll stay to help you with the Payne order, to show you what a good guy I really am.'

'Did you come up with that on the spur of the moment, or were you planning it all along?' She looked at him suspiciously, and he grinned.

'I'd planned it all along. I had absolutely no confidence in you taking the day off, and since I have nothing better to do myself except spend more time at the shop, I thought I'd drop by to give you a hand.'

'There's a lot of work to be done on your house. You could get started on that.'

'I wanted to talk to you about that, I'd like your advice. But let's have some lunch first. You have a can opener somewhere?'

After soup and sandwiches, they sat in the living room and began to stick pins into holes to the soothing tones of a Mozart piano concerto. Brand eyed the box warily.

'How many more do we have to do?'

'I don't know. I quit counting a long time ago. I sort of go into a trance, doing this, and after a while I don't know I'm doing it any more, it's so automatic.' She studied the pile of little bags. 'I think if we do a couple of hours today and I do a couple of hours tomorrow, we can probably finish the rest at the workshop on Monday if I get some help.'

He viewed the boxes with some speculation. 'Have you done all the rest by yourself, except what Sally did on Tuesday and Wednesday?

She shook her head. 'I had a lot of help from a friend. He came Monday and Tuesday night and helped me.'

He looked at her with narrowed eyes. 'What kind of a friend?'

She shrugged lightly. 'He lives down the road. He brought me vegetables from his garden this summer and he helped me fix some things around the house. We go to a movie sometimes, and he offers to share a frozen pizza on a regular basis.'

'Sounds cosy,' he said drily.

Briana bent to her work and for a while they were silent, each absorbed in their own thoughts. Briana wondered about Christa. Brand had never talked about her.

'Somebody mentioned Christa yesterday,' she ventured, not knowing what his reaction would be.

He looked up, his face calm. 'Christa and I knew each other for a long time, since high school. Our parents were friends in Washington.'

Maybe Christa had been a spoiled little rich girl. It was an interesting thought, but not one she could express in discreet terms. 'Were you planning to marry her?'

'I think that was the general idea. It didn't work out.' He paused, looking into her eyes. 'I was too absorbed in the workshop and the people, and Christa was too absorbed in herself. She wanted more than I was capable of giving at the time. The two of us just didn't click together, no matter what we really felt for each other. If you ever wondered where I got my antipathy for spoiled little rich girls, then now you know. She wanted all the shine and glitter of life, as she had always been used to. She had no real understanding of my work, and why it was so important to me. She didn't really care. I resented that deeply.'

'But you loved her.'

'I thought I did.' He gave a lopsided little smile. 'I don't want to put all the blame on her, though. In my own way I was very selfish, too. I didn't give her much time or attention. I expected too much from her. After all, there was no good reason why my obsession should also be hers. In the end it all fell apart. She walked out on me.'

He dropped the metal part he was still holding in his hand back in the box and picked up another. For a while they worked in silence. Briana thought of Christa, trying to imagine their relationship, but giving up. Her thoughts began to wander. She wondered about her parents in Tokyo, about Christmas and what presents to buy, about finally doing something to the house to make it her own.

'Have you ever really looked at these things?' Brand asked suddenly, studying the little metal part in his hand. 'I haven't the faintest idea what it's for, what function it has in these machines.' He turned the thing over in his hand, looking at it from all sides. 'I invented a little gismo like this some years ago. Something you can look at and not have any idea what it is. It's a very simple little thing, a safety device for those electric saws we use in the workshop.'

Briana looked at him with interest. 'You invented a safety device? I didn't know that. How did you do that?'

He shrugged. 'We were training some young boys to work with the saws when we first started the shop. I was doing it myself, actually, together with a friend. It was obvious, as we saw the boys work, that we needed better precautions. It wasn't as safe to work with these saws as we had originally assumed. I kept mulling it over in my mind, I kept trying different things. The last thing I wanted was to have an accident in my shop.' He dropped the part in the box and picked up another one from the pile, working absently, his mind on the story he was telling.

'One night at home it just occurred to me. I was eating a ham sandwich and watching TV—don't ask me why I remember that, but I do—and whammo, the solution was there in my head. I knew exactly what to do.' He looked up and grinned. 'It was after nine in the evening and I'd just come home from the shop and . . .'

Briana nodded. 'You got in your car and went back to the shop to work on it.'

'I stayed up all night trying to get the design right. The next day I went to a friend who had a machine shop and we actually managed to make a real one we could use. It worked like a charm.'

'Was it something that could have wider applications? Did you get a patent?'

His mouth quirked. 'You're so smart. You don't miss a beat, do you? Yes, I got the patent and then I sold it to a manufacturer.' He grinned boyishly, pausing for a moment. 'For a bundle.'

That explained a few things. 'Hence your nice old house,' Briana concluded. 'And the group home.'

His eyes narrowed. 'Who told you about the group home?'

She raised her eyebrows in surprise. 'Isn't it common knowledge?'

'No,' he said shortly. 'Who told you?'

'One of your friends, yesterday. He assumed I knew.'

He frowned. 'I see. Well, I don't want it to get around.'

'All right, I won't mention it.' She pulled out another pin, reversed it and pushed it back in. She looked at him covertly, seeing a ray of sunshine pick out the red highlights in his hair. He hadn't liked the idea of her knowing about the group home. He didn't want anyone to know. She had to admire him for that. No matter how despotically he reigned over the shop, he wasn't out for personal glory.

Briana offered to give him dinner, but he didn't want to hear of it. 'You've done enough cooking for a while. Let's eat out.'

Briana didn't mind in the least. Getting out of the house was a good idea having been cooped up all day with the pins and holes. It was strange to think that the man who'd haughtily told her there was no way in the world he was ever going to hire her was now in her living-room helping her. In the last two days, they'd spent more time together than all the times added up together in the last few months. Being alone with him for such an extended time had proved to be interesting. They'd talked about his childhood, hers, about his plans for the house. He'd asked her opinion and then, to her surprise, he'd asked her to go with him on Saturday and buy a carpet and furniture.

By the time they'd finished their dinner, she was amazed they'd spent all those hours alone without an angry word. It was still early as they drove home and she wasn't sure if she should ask him in, and if she did would he consider it an invitation? There wasn't any doubt that he'd want to come in, so how was she going to keep him out? She considered various approaches, practising a number of lines. *I'm really tired*, she'd say casually, *I think I'll go to bed early tonight*. No, too obvious. *Stay in the car, I can manage*. No, equally obvious. *Please don't come in. I don't want to go to bed with you*. Blunt, but true. No, she corrected herself, not true. A lie of some magnitude, actually. There was nothing she wanted more than to make love with Brand, glorious, passionate, abandoned love. *Please, don't come in. I'm terrified of making another mistake*. Now that was the naked truth.

She sighed deeply and Brand gave her a quick amused look.

'Problems?'

'No, no. I'm tired, I guess. It was so late last night. I'm not used to that any more.' She covered up a yawn that appeared spontaneously and expediently. Well, it was, after all, not a lie. She *was* tired.

He gave her a crooked smile. 'My fault, I suppose, keeping you even later than was necessary.'

He slowed the car and came to a stop in front of the house, got out and came around to open her door.

Keys in hand, she walked up to the house, Brand following. 'Thanks very much for all your help today, and for dinner of course,' she said, putting her key in the lock.

With his hands on her shoulders he turned her towards him. 'You don't want to ask me in, do you?' He sounded amused.

She feigned a bright smile. 'Actually, I was thinking of going to bed early and sleeping late.'

'Alone, I take it?'

'Yes.'

'It's only postponing the inevitable, you know.'

'I hadn't thought of it,' she returned lightly.

'Liar,' he said softly. His arms came around her and drew her close, his mouth almost touching hers. 'I'll let you get away with it tonight, because I know you really are tired, but next time I may not be so understanding.' His lips brushed hers, teasing, tantalising. She turned her face away.

'You take a lot for granted, don't you?'

'Such as what?'

'That I want to sleep with you.'

'Oh, but you do,' he said softly, kissing her behind her ear. 'I have foolproof instincts that way. I just don't think you have convinced yourself yet. I'm sure I can help.'

'Your arrogance leaves me speechless. Now let me go. I want to go inside.'

He didn't let go, but found her mouth and kissed her in such a blatantly erotic way that her blood rushed to her head. Then he released her abruptly and smiled at her smugly.

'That'll give you something to dream about. Good night, Briana.' And with that he strode down the path to the car.

He came for her at noon the next day to go shopping for rugs, curtains and furniture. The showroom they visited was as vast as a football field. They argued over colours, prices, styles and materials. Briana was having a wonderful time.

'Why are you being so difficult?' Brand moaned. 'I like that chair.'

'But it's the wrong colour!'

'But I like that colour!'

'So do I, but it won't go with the other colours in that room. It'll look all wrong!' She smiled conspiratorially at the salesman, who stood by their side, seemingly patient. He was a colourless little man, slightly seedy around the edges, with a pasty-looking face.

Brand glared at her. 'Whose house is this anyway? Yours or mine?'

She wondered what the salesman might think of

that question. He'd pinned them down as a young married couple furnishing their new house. She smiled sweetly at Brand. 'Yours, of course. But since you asked my advice, I'm dispensing it. I didn't come along with you this afternoon to watch you make stupid mistakes and then get blamed for it when you decided it was all wrong after it was too late.'

'This chair comes in different colours,' the salesman interjected hastily, trying to avoid a full-scale war in his showroom. 'Let me get you the sample book.'

In the end they always agreed, their tastes not really all that different.

'You look as if you're enjoying this,' Brand said, surveying her suspiciously.

She smiled sunnily. 'Shouldn't I? I've never yet furnished a house. It's good practice for when I do my own. I keep telling myself I'm going to do that one of these days.'

'Why bother? You can move in with me. You should like it, you picked all this stuff out yourself.'

'I did not! I advised and you decided.'

'You made sure I decided what you advised.'

'Are you accusing me of manipulating?'

'Never!'

'Good, I didn't think so. You're basically an intelligent man. You know that good advice is only beneficial if you follow it.'

Brand groaned and turned to the salesman, this one tall and thin with sparks in his eyes. 'What am I going to do with her?' he asked.

'Leave her home next time,' the salesman suggested.

They had a leisurely dinner in a Greek restaurant, then drove back to Leesburg, arguing some more. They drove down Loudoun Street, past the library, the hospital. He was taking her to his own house. Fearful anticipation began to churn in her stomach. She'd been expecting this. It had been in her mind all day and it was no use denying it. The whole afternoon had been leading up to it—the vibrations between them, the looks, the smiles. He was taking her to his house expecting her to stay the night with him.

'Aren't you taking me home?' she asked unnecessarily.

'It's still early, not even nine. Did you want to go home?' It was asked in such a normal, level, reasonable tone that she couldn't think of any way to answer it affirmatively without sounding like a frightened virgin.

'Not particularly. I just assumed that that's where we were going.' She tried to sound as casual as possible and she wondered why she seemed to have this lack of confidence and assuredness. Why couldn't she just put her foot down? *Listen, I don't intend to sleep with you. Just take me home.* She hadn't had a problem with the other men she'd known in the last year. She hadn't been interested in any of them, which made everything a foregone conclusion. With Brand she simply had no strength to resist. Was she fighting him, or herself?

Maybe she was misreading him. Maybe he'd offer her a drink and take her home later.

Sure, sure, she derided herself, dream on.

'How about another cup of coffee?' he suggested after they'd gone inside. 'Or a little eggnog?'

'I'll have a little eggnog.'

'I'll build us a fire. Sit down. Don't stand there like a forlorn little waif. I'll be right back.'

Sipping the eggnog, she watched him arrange paper, kindling and logs on the grate. In no time at all he had a roaring fire and he grinned at her with boyish delight.

'I do like building fires. Come, sit with me.' He patted the rug in front of the fire. 'You look frozen. Are you cold?'

'Yes.' It was the truth. She got up from the chair

and lowered herself on the rug next to him, his nearness doing her peace of mind no good at all. They sipped their drinks, watching the dancing flames.

'You're not saying anything,' he said at last. 'Why are you so nervous? Are you afraid I'm going to seduce you?'

'Well, you are!'

He laughed. 'I would like not to have to. I'd prefer this to be a ... eh ... joint venture, so to speak.' He frowned. 'Scratch that. I'd like it to be a mutual adventure into sensuous pleasures and passionate delights.' He grinned at her, pleased with himself.

She laughed. 'That does sound better.'

'I thought so. He took the glass from her and deposited it on the table. 'Now, come here.' He held her close. 'Stop being so tense.'

She let out a deep sigh. 'I'm having a lot of trouble with this.'

'I can tell. You're worried about getting hurt again.'

'Something like that.'

'I'd say exactly like that.' He was looking at her face, smiling faintly. A minute or so passed, then slowly he bent his face to hers and kissed her gently. 'I love you,' he said quietly. 'I really do.'

'I love you too,' she heard herself say in a panicky little voice. Her body began to tremble. Oh, God, what was the matter with her? She *had* to stop this. She put her arms around his neck, searched for his mouth. 'Kiss me,' she whispered, 'hold me.'

He kissed her gently, then drew away, his face serious. 'Briana, I want you to tell me about your husband, about your marriage.'

'I don't want to.'

'I think you should.'

At first the words wouldn't come, yet she knew that, deep down, she wanted him to know how it had been with her and Cliff. She wanted to tell him everything, the story of her marriage, the sordid betrayal, the disillusionment, the nightmare that followed and lasted for a year. She wished it wouldn't matter any more, that it should make no difference, but you couldn't erase an experience like that out of your mind and not be influenced by it.

'He said he loved me,' she said at last. It seemed to be the key. She had believed him, and maybe he had even believed it himself. It's what she could never understand—the fact that he so easily had disposed of that love, that it had meant so little to him. Her face rested against Brand's chest. It was easier to talk without looking at him. 'And I loved him.' She swallowed painfully. 'But it wasn't enough. There were other women—I didn't know.' Then the words came tumbling out. She told him everything, talking into his chest, glad for the comfort of his arms around her.

'One day I came home from shopping and found him in bed . . . in *our* bed, with some girl. I thought . . . I would die right there.'

His arms tightened around her. 'Go on.'

'He told me he was bored with me. He said . . .' Her voice shook so badly she could barely go on. 'He said I . . . I was no good in bed.'

She heard his sharp intake of breath. 'The bastard!' he said with so much venom that it almost frightened her. He drew back and lifted her face away from his chest.

She looked at him, giving a rueful smile. 'He just said it to hurt me.'

'But you believed him?'

'Oh, I wondered about it, in the beginning. I was devastated and I tried to explain it all. Sometimes I did ask myself if I wasn't at fault somehow. But later I realised that there was something wrong with him, not with me. He always had women around him before we were married. I was so naive. I thought if I loved him enough, he wouldn't need them any more. Well, I was wrong.'

'And now you don't trust other men.'

'Another relationship scares me. I've been avoiding it.'

'We're not all like him, Briana.'

'I know that. But my self-confidence is a bit shaky.' I was so blind, it frightens me.'

'I don't believe you're blind when it comes to me,' he said and there was humour in his voice. 'You've already informed me of all my flaws and defects.'

And running around with a lot of women wasn't one of them. Brand was no Cliff. When Brand believed in something, he stuck by it, no matter what the difficulties. His priorities were clear. And he said he loved her.

His mouth moved seductively over her temple, her cheek, her chin. Her mouth was eager for his when his lips touched hers. His back was warm and strong under her hands and she felt heady with his nearness. His hand began to move gently, softly over her body, sliding under her clothes, caressing her skin, her breasts. A quiver ran down her back.

'Briana,' he muttered, 'I want you so much, so much.' She grew still in his arms. She felt the heavy beating of his heart, heard his rapid breathing.

'What's the matter?' he whispered.

'I don't know . . .' She shrugged lightly. 'Nothing.'

He raised his head, smiling into her eyes. 'Are you worried about what Cliff said to you?'

She shook her head. 'I don't think so. But . . . it's been a long time,' she said with difficulty.

He laughed softly. 'Don't worry about it. It's like riding a bike. You never forget.'

She looked into his eyes and mirth got the better of her. She began to laugh. 'Oh, Brand!'

He drew her close. 'Oh, Brand what?' he said in her ear. 'Oh, Brand, please take me upstairs? Oh, Brand, please make love to me? Oh, Brand, please . . .'

She squirmed in his arms, laughing. 'Stop it!'

'Not on your life. Come on. He jumped up, taking her hand. They walked up the stairs, to the bedroom where she'd changed her clothes the day before. Night blue carpeting, a big bed covered with a blue and white quilt.

Brand closed the door, leaned against it, smiling faintly, and looked at her with smouldering eyes.

CHAPTER NINE

'DON'T look at me like that!' she said. 'And don't lean against that door as if you're holding me captive!'

'Sorry.' He laughed, moving away from the door and taking her in his arms. 'I am rather happy to finally have you here though,' he whispered in her ear. 'Now, what's your desire?'

'I think I'd like another drink. And a shower. And I want to go home.'

'Ah, I sense delaying tactics. No go. You're staying right here.' He grinned wolfishly.

'You love it, don't you, this great seduction routine?'

He said nothing, the look in his eyes eloquent.

'Why didn't you just do it downstairs? On the rug in front of the fire? Isn't that supposed to be more romantic?'

He shook his head. 'The rug is too small, the floor too hard. I like the comfort of a big bed, unimaginative as that may seem.' He came towards her, put his arm around her and searched for the zipper in her dress. She twisted away.

'You asked me what my desire was. I want a shower and a drink.'

'You don't want to go home any more? Good. We're making progress. You can have the drink and the shower as long as you keep it short. Otherwise I'll come in and help you. I'm good at soaping, especially.'

'No, thanks.'

He was kissing her neck. 'What kind of drink? Tomato juice?'

'A double whiskey, neat.'

'Not a chance, baby. You'll be comatose by the time you finish it.'

She smiled. 'That's the whole idea.'

'No, it isn't. It won't be any fun that way. I'd like you relatively sober while I take you down the path of primitive passion and pleasure.' He began to unzip her dress, sliding it over her shoulders. He kissed her hairline, her earlobe, her throat, and sweet excitement softly swirled inside her. She could feel the change in him, a sudden tense eagerness.

'Now get ready,' he whispered, 'and I'll get us a drink.'

He was gone long enough for her to finish in the bathroom. She was sitting on the edge of the bed, wrapped in a dry towel when he came in. She'd considered getting into the bed, but the idea made her uneasy. It was a strange bed. She wasn't even sure she really wanted to be in it, to go through with this. She'd make love with him just once and she'd be lost. Well, a little voice said, you're lost already.

He handed her a glass. 'Give me a couple of minutes.' He disappeared into the bathroom.

A couple of minutes. Long enough to get dressed and get out of there. And then what? Walk home down the deserted country roads? Grow up, she told herself. You want to make love, so make love. She gulped down the drink, which was her usual tomato juice with a little vodka added. She got up and switched off the light, leaving on only the small bedside lamp.

He came back into the room, a towel around his waist. He sat down next to her, pushing her gently down on to the bed. His face was close to hers. 'What about precautions?' he asked softly. 'You want me to take care of it?'

She had not expected him to raise the issue and his concern warmed her. She shook her head. 'No, it's all right. I . . . thanks for offering.'

A half-smile tugged at his mouth. He took the towel

from around her body and tossed it on the floor, then took off his own. He bent his face to hers, brushing his lips softly over her mouth.

'Forget everything,' he said softly, stroking her hair, playing with the curls. 'Just relax.'

She closed her eyes, feeling a rush of desire as she felt his warm body against her on the bed. He kissed her gently all over, moving his mouth softly against her skin. His hand was sliding over her belly, her thighs. 'You're beautiful,' he said softly. 'I like the feel of you.'

Her body sprang alive to his touch, her senses quivering with the delight of it. Slowly she raised one arm and ran her hands through his hair, down his neck. She fingered the muscles of his neck, his shoulders, slid her hand down to the small of his back. He moved slightly and her hand fell away from his body.

'Don't stop,' Brand whispered. 'It feels good.' He lifted her hand and placed it on his thigh. With hammering heart, she moved her hand up, the urge to touch him suddenly overwhelming. She wanted to love him and please him and make him happy. Moving on to her side, she pressed herself closer. He kept on stroking her as she found his mouth and kissed him, kissed him with a fire leaping up inside her, kissed him deeply without any thought of anything. A low, soft sound came from his throat and she felt a tremor go through his body. Her hand moved over him, searching, touching, teasing. His mouth moved down her body, kissing her breast, her stomach, until suddenly all was lost in a frenzy of motion. There was no rational thought, no fear as they moved together in mutual rapture until the tension broke with a dizzying force that left them breathless and sated.

She lay still, heart racing alarmingly, hiding her face in his shoulder. For a long time they lay in silence, not moving, then he began to kiss her neck, her shoulder with featherlike touches of his lips.

'Briana?' he asked.

'What?'

'That was wonderful.'

'Really?' The eagerness in her voice embarrassed her.

His body shook with laughter. 'What else would you call it?'

'I don't know.'

'You don't know?' He bit her earlobe gently. 'How can you not know? Seemed to me you enjoyed it quite considerably.'

'You know *I* did,' she muttered into his shoulder. 'I just don't know about you.'

'I just told you it was wonderful and you'd better believe me. You're sexy and sensuous and seductive and you made me feel very, very, very good.'

'I'm glad.'

'Come on, stop hiding. I want to see your face.'

'No.'

'Briana!'

She stayed where she was.

'Briana! Look at me!' he ordered.

She didn't move. He nudged against her shoulder, tickled her neck, blew in her ear, until she began to squirm to avoid his teasing hands and mouth. He whispered erotic nonsense in her ear until she could contain herself no longer and began to laugh, still avoiding looking at him. He began to wrestle with her so she had no choice but to move in order to defend herself. They rolled around in the bed, laughing, breathless, finally stopping out of sheer exhaustion. Arms and legs wrapped around each other, they lay caught in the twisted sheets, breathing hard.

'You don't play fair,' she complained.

'In love and war everything is fair.' He moved a little closer, his hand trailing up her thigh.

'You're too big, and too strong,' she moaned, trying to move away from his exploring hand.

He gave a lewd grin. 'That makes it more fun to wrestle with naked ladies.'

'And it isn't fair that you're not ticklish!'

'Complaints, complaints. And I *am* ticklish, just not all over.'

'So where *are* you ticklish?'

His eyes gleamed. 'That's for me to know and for you to find out.'

She sniffed haughtily. 'Well, if you're not telling, I'm going to sleep.' She turned her back to him, pulling away as much of the sheet and quilt as she could, and closed her eyes. For a while nothing happened. Then he moved over to her side of the bed and lay against her back, curling around her, one hand gently covering her breast.

'I love you,' he whispered in her ear. 'I love your body and I love what you do to me.'

Her heart swelled with love. 'Me too,' she returned, her voice husky with emotion. Feeling happy and contented, she lay half-dozing, half-dreaming, aware of his hand warm and intimate on her breast.

She was alone when she awoke the next morning. Brand, where was Brand? Disappointment made her sigh. She looked around the semi-dark room. Grey light struggled in through a crack in the curtains. Yuk, another dreary day outside. Raising herself up on one elbow, she looked at the digital clock on the bedside table. 9:33. Good work. She stretched luxuriously in the big bed, smiling to herself. Brand had probably been up for hours. The thought of him alone made her grow warm all over. Maybe she should get up and find him. Maybe she should stay in bed. It was awfully comfortable.

She was still contemplating the plusses and minuses of the decision when the door opened and Brand came in with a big tray loaded with food. He was wearing a short, blue terry-cloth robe and his hair was uncombed. The gleam in his eyes as they met hers made her pulse race. She felt a rush of longing to be in his arms again. He set the tray down on a small table, which he then picked up and placed next to the bed within easy reach.

'I thought you'd never wake up,' he accused. 'I was coming to give you a little help.'

Briana surveyed the tray. There was enough food there to last them for three days. 'What is all this?' she asked in amazement.

'Croissants, hot from the oven. Bagels and cream cheese. Blueberry muffins, also warm. Three kinds of doughnuts. Butter, jam, grapefruit juice and coffee,' he enumerated. 'And of course the Sunday paper. I'll get it right now.' He was out of the room and back in less than a minute and deposited the heavy load of paper on the bed, grinning at her and looking satisfied with himself.

'Could I possibly persuade you to stay in bed with me for the rest of the morning?'

Briana frowned at the loaded tray. 'You weren't expecting any guests for breakfast, by any chance?'

There was a devilish glint in his eyes. 'Only one.'

'You were really sure of yourself, weren't you?'

He smiled smugly. 'It's a habit of mine.' He took off his robe and climbed back into bed. 'Now, before I pour us some coffee, I want to give you a proper ravishing.'

'A ravishing? There's no such thing.'

'Oh, no?' he taunted, gathering her up close against him.

'No.' She squirmed as he ran his tongue along the edge of her ear. 'I'll bet you there's no such word in the dictionary.'

'What do they know?' He blew in her ear. 'Let me educate you.'

Monday was a strange day. She saw Brand on a couple

of occasions and he greeted her in his normal boss
fashion and she felt like hitting him. Well, what had
she expected? That he hugged and kissed her in front
of everybody? She sighed. If only he wasn't so
hopelessly authoritarian!

All Sunday morning they'd spent in bed, eating,
reading, fighting over the various sections of the
paper. Making love again. She would have cheerfully
stayed with him for the rest of the day had Brand not
had other obligations. His parents and Tammy were
returning from New Hampshire and he was picking
them up from the airport and taking them out to
dinner later on.

'I'll see you at the shop on Monday,' he said, kissing
her goodbye. Well, here they were at the shop and he
had dropped his lover mode and was back into his boss
routine. She wondered when she'd see him again
outside of work. Tonight there was a board meeting,
so that was out. Maybe she should invite him to
dinner at her house tomorrow night. Fix a gourmet
meal. Something sensuously exotic. Her mind began
to mull over the various possibilities, her hands busy
with the last of the Payne order parts.

Help had arrived in the form of Mrs Stamford, Jill's
mother, who had helped out before on various
occasions, and one of the girls from the kitchen. The
Payne order was finished by mid-afternoon and by the
time Briana went home the boxes were ready for
delivery. She'd never before been so happy to see a job
finished. A sore throat had plagued her all afternoon
and her body felt achy. Sally had asked if she felt all
right. 'You look pale, you know. Like you sick or
sumpin,' she'd said, and Tammy had nodded in
agreement.

Please don't let me come down with something, she
prayed silently as she drove home. She'd take some
aspirin, go to bed early for a change.

The phone rang just as she was eating some left-over spaghetti. It was Ross. As she heard his voice she suddenly remembered he had promised to come by.

'I'm sorry I didn't call you earlier,' he said, sounding rather distracted. 'I promised to come by and help you with that order, but to tell you the truth it totally escaped me. We had a minor disaster here and I'm still in Maryland.'

'What happened?'

'My mother broke her leg. She'll be all right, but I think I'll stay for couple of days and help out. How's the order coming along?'

'It's all finished, don't worry about it. I'm sorry about your mother. How did it happen?'

He talked to her for a while longer and after she'd hung up she finished eating, watched a little TV and got into bed.

The next morning she surfaced from sleep, feeling wretched. Her throat hurt, her head ached. She struggled out of bed, swallowed some aspirin and got ready for work. It did not get any better during the day. Her mood suffered and her workers were rather subdued. 'You're not-not-not f-f-f-feeling well, are you?' Jill said, looking worried. Everyone seemed to be working extra hard, trying to be as helpful as was possible. Sally poured her coffee. Jim was more quiet than he'd ever been. It was amazing to see how much her mood and feelings affected the behaviour of her workers.

By night she felt worse. She made a hot toddy with lemon, honey and tea and took a cold capsule before going to bed at the ridiculous hour of eight.

She struggled through the days, living on hot toddies, orange juice, cold capsules and feeling steadily worse. The sympathy of her workers made her feel guilty. Her sore throat was gone, but her nose started running and her head was congested, giving her headaches. Brand was out of the office for most of Tuesday and Wednesday and she'd seen little of him, which was just as well. He came into her workroom on Thursday, took one look at her and told her to go home.

'I'm all right, it's just a cold,' she said carelessly.

He frowned impatiently. 'You've got the 'flu! You're not fit to stand on your legs, for heaven's sake!'

'Why don't you let me decide?' she snapped, turning away from him and continuing with her work as if he weren't there.

She couldn't afford to be sick with all these people depending on her. As long as it wasn't any more serious than a cold she'd just have to suffer through it. It would take its own good time to ravage her body and then move on.

'Don't be such a stubborn idiot!' he said in a voice so low only she could hear. 'I'll call Mrs Stamford. She can take over for a couple of days. She's done it before.'

'It's not necessary!' she hissed. 'I'm doing fine.' Having said that, a coughing spell overtook her. The cold had gradually descended into her chest and had apparently settled in firmly. It took several minutes before she had herself calmed down.

'Just fine, I can tell,' he said sarcastically. 'Choking cough, nasal congestion, watery eyes, rotten colour. Absolutely wonderful.'

'Oh, get lost!' she said emphatically. 'I don't need your warm and well-meant commiseration. Just leave me alone!'

'My pleasure.' He turned on his heel and strode out of the room.

She glanced at her watch. Ten past three. Less than an hour and a half before everyone would leave. She could make it. As soon as she got home she'd make a hot toddy and crawl into bed. It was a soothing thought. She tried not to think about the sight of the unmade bed. It had been days since she'd last made it; getting out of it alone taking all the strength she had in the mornings. Better get some cough syrup at the store first. One more thing to add to the rather impressive array of home-cure medicine she had collected already.

In the store she found that even buying cough syrup involved making decisions these days. She stared dispiritedly at the selection of potions on display. What kind did she need? What kind of cough did she have? A rotten cough is what I have, she thought angrily, taking a bottle off the shelf. She stood in line at the cash register, coughing miserably, wondering why she always ended up in the slowest line.

Apparently the syrup did help. She was sound asleep when a loud, insistent knocking woke her and she dragged herself out of bed. Pulling on her robe, she stumbled through the living-room into the kitchen to open the back door.

'Good God,' Ross said as he entered the kitchen. 'Were you in bed? Are you sick?' He closed the door behind him.

'Just a cold,' she said, shivering.

'You look like hell.'

'Thanks, I needed that.' She turned and walked into the living room, dropped herself down on the couch, wrapping the afghan around herself. She ran a hand over her hair, which was standing out in all directions in its usual after-sleep fashion. She didn't care what she looked like.

'Why is it so cold in here?' Ross asked, looking at her with a frown.

'I don't know. I guess I forgot to turn up the stove when I came home. I went straight to bed.'

Ross knelt in front of the oil stove, examining it for a moment before turning it up. 'Is there anything I can do?' he asked as he straightened. 'Have you had dinner?'

She shook her head, swallowing at the tickling sensation in her throat and chest. 'I'm ... I'm not hungry.' A coughing fit racked her body. Leaning forward she tried to stop the spasms, but she had no control over them. Tears ran down her cheeks. 'Oh, God,' she gasped, 'I hate this!' She took the box of tissues Ross offered her and wiped her eyes and blew her nose. It seemed ages before she'd calmed down and could breathe normally again. She looked up at Ross. He was standing in the middle of the room, poised as if ready to call an ambulance.

'Don't look so worried. I'm not dying, even though it does seem like it.'

'I don't like the sound of that cough.'

'I thought it was rather tuneful myself.'

'When did this start?'

'The coughing? Just today. I'vc had a cold since Monday. Sore throat, nasal congestion, headache, all the usual symptoms.'

'Have you seen a doctor?'

'A doctor? What for? It's just a cold. I don't even have a fever.'

'If that cough gets any worse, you'd better see a doctor.'

'It can't possibly get worse, and please don't act like a worried mother. I'll be fine.' She shivered again and drew the afghan closer around her.

'When did you eat last?'

'Ross! Stop it! If you really want to do something, make me a hot toddy, please. Squeeze out a lemon, add hot tea and honey. It's all on the kitchen work-surface.'

She closed her eyes and leaned her head back, listening to the sounds coming from the kitchen. Water running, the clinking of china and cutlery. Then the whistling of the tea kettle. The kitchen was a disaster. Dirty dishes all over the place. She hadn't washed anything for days, merely rinsed the plates and cups and left them in the sink. She hadn't really eaten much lately. Her appetite was gone and the effort of cooking anything had seemed pointless.

Ross came back into the room carrying a tray with two cups and a jar of honey. 'Taste it and see if it's sweet enough.' He put the tray on the coffee table, taking off a cup of coffee he'd made for himself.

She took her mug and sipped the hot brew. 'Just right. Thanks.'

'You should have stayed with your parents in Florida,' he said, looking at her with concern in his eyes.

'Florida? Oh, yes.' She shrugged. 'I didn't go to Florida.' She might as well tell him now. Lying wasn't one of her strong points and it was usually more trouble than it was worth.

'What do you mean you didn't go to Florida? You said you were going home for Thanksgiving?' He looked genuinely surprised.

'I was, but something happened at the last moment. My mother called to say my father had to go to Japan pronto and she was going with him and she wanted me to come too.' She sighed. 'I couldn't, of course. So I stayed here.'

'You stayed here?' The blue eyes looked at her suspiciously. 'When did she call you?'

'I don't remember. Monday or Tuesday.'

Anger leaped in his eyes. 'Why didn't you say something? You could have come home with me! You would have been more than welcome!'

'I know, Ross, but I already had another invitation.'

Ross paced restless through the room. 'Who?'

'Brand Edwards. He had a dinner party at his house and he asked me to help him with the turkey.'

Ross slowly turned to look at her. '*Brand Edwards?* You've got to be kidding!'

'I'm not. I hadn't planned to take him up on it, but he came past my house at eleven on Wednesday night, saw the light on and became suspicious, thinking I was away.' She grimaced wryly. 'He found me sticking little pins in little holes and demanded to know what was going on. Then he said he wanted me to come and have Thanksgiving dinner at his house. He came by the next morning and practically dragged me out of bed.'

'So like a good little girl you went,' he said without inflection.

'He was rather in need of help.' She couldn't help smiling. 'He'd never cooked a turkey before and he'd invited ten people. It was quite a nice day, actually.'

Ross looked at her with narrowed eyes. 'I thought you couldn't stand the man.'

'Away from the shop he's ... like a different person.' Oh, God, she wished this conversation were over.

'I see.' He stared at the flower arrangement on the table. It was beginning to look rather dead and dry. It was time to throw it out. 'From him?' he asked.

Briana nodded, unable to speak as she fought the approach of another coughing attack. It was not to be warded off. For the next few minutes, her body struggled with the coughing convulsions, the rasping sound of them coming from deep in her chest. Tears streamed down her face and her hands pressed against her breasts.

Limp as a rag doll, she slumped against the back of the couch when it was finally over. She felt drained of all strength.

Ross uttered a profanity. 'Have you been taking anything for this?'

'Yes. The bottle is in the bathroom. I'd better have some more, or I'll never sleep tonight.'

'I'll get it.'

Obediently she opened her mouth when he fed her the syrup from a spoon, feeling like a child and not minding it.

'And now you'd better get back to bed. Come on.' He took her arm and led her back to her room. Taking her robe off, she crawled back under the covers, shivering. 'I need some flannel sheets. This cold is beastly.' She attempted a smile. 'Thanks for helping me. You'd better get out of here before you catch the bug too.'

'Do you need anything else? I can go to the store if you like.'

She shook her head. 'No, all I want is sleep. Just lock the back door and go out the front. That one locks itself.'

'I'll check up in the morning and see how you are.' He left the bedroom and she closed her eyes, burrowing deeper under the covers. Faintly she heard him move around, then the running of water and the sound of dishes and cutlery. She groaned. He was washing the dishes! She began to cough again and buried her face in the pillow to muffle the sound. Exhausted, she eventually fell asleep.

At some point in the night she woke up, flushed and warm and with a terrible thirst. She got up to find a drink of water and her head began to spin with dizziness as she came to her feet. Oh, great, she thought, now I have a fever too. She drank a glass of water, swallowed a couple of aspirin and some more cough syrup. Holding on the walls, she found her way back to bed. Coughing wretchedly she lay awake for more than an hour before sleep overtook her again.

It was almost seven when she awoke again, feeling even worse. There was no doubt she was running a temperature. She couldn't go to work. She couldn't stand on her legs without practically falling over. The only thing to do was call Brand and let him know. Grimacing, she pulled on her robe and staggered into the living room and searched through the phone directory for his home number. Strange that she didn't even know that. Shivering, she dialled, praying she wouldn't have another fit of coughing while she talked to him. No such luck. She'd barely mentioned her name when an uncontrollable coughing spasm took over her voice. 'I'm sorry,' she wheezed. 'I . . . I can't . . .' It was impossible to talk.

Brand swore into her ear. 'You've got it bad, right? Okay, okay, don't say anything. Get back into bed. I'll see you later.' He hung up. Briana did the same, groping for the box of tissues on the coffee table. Oh, damn, she thought, how long is this going to go on? She went into the kitchen to make a cup of tea, finding all the dishes done and everything neatly put away.

Less then fifteen minutes later, the doorbell rang. For a moment she considered letting it ring, but she knew it was Brand and he'd probably find his way in one way or another.

She opened the door, greeting him with a hacking cough. He came in, closed the door behind him and gave her a frowning look as he listened to her cough.

'You'd better put some clothes on. I'm taking you to the doctor.'

'I—don't—need—a—doctor,' she gasped. 'It's just a cold!'

He advanced towards her and put his hand on her forehead. She gasped. 'Your hand is cold!'

'You've got a fever, lady. And if my guess is any good, a case of bronchitis, which needs to be looked at.' The tone of his voice left no room for objection. 'You have a doctor here?'

She shook her head.

'I didn't think so. I'll take you to Fielding, our family doctor. I already called and he can see you in half an hour, so don't waste any time getting ready.' He took her arm and propelled her out of the room into her bedroom.

'Good God,' he said, looking around the room. 'What a disaster area.'

'What I need is criticism right now,' she said sarcastically. 'Just leave me alone. I need to take a shower.' She clutched her chest, feeling new spasms coming up. He took her robe and slid it off her shoulders as a violent cough seized her.

He shook his head in dismay. 'Briana! How can you say this is just a cold? Don't you *hear* yourself?'

She couldn't reply, just gasped for air between coughs.

'I'm going to turn on the shower. I'll be right back.' Which he was. 'Come on,' he directed, taking her arm and leading her to the bathroom. 'Now take off that nightgown and get in.'

'Listen, I'm capable of taking a shower by myself! I don't need your tender ministrations.'

He didn't even answer. His hands reached out and slipped the straps of her nightgown over her shoulders and it slid to the floor. Reaching for the shower curtain with one hand, he gently nudged her towards it. A furious accusation reached her throat but got no further as she began to cough again. Gasping, she stepped in the shower stall, closing the curtain and leaning weakly against the tile wall. When she had recovered she reached for her shower cap and put it on. Her hair would have to wait for another time. She felt wretched. She hoped she could stand up long enough to wash and rinse herself. She felt like she might crumble in a heap on the shower cubicle floor and drown.

Conscious of him close by in the small room, she began to wash quickly, asking him to hand her a towel when she was finished. Wrapping it around herself, she stepped out of the shower. He was leaning against the door, giving her a faintly amused look.

'I've always wondered what you'd look like in a yellow shower cap,' he said.

'Oh, shut up,' she snapped. 'Haven't you ever heard of the concept of privacy?'

'You're a wreck, lady,' he said without emotion. 'I'm not having you slip or do something fatal to yourself while you're in here alone.' He straightened away from the door and opened it to let her out. 'I'll wait in the living-room while you get dressed. And be quick now, we don't have much time.'

'Slave-driver,' she muttered under her breath as she slipped passed him.

'I heard that,' he answered drily, and she had the childish impulse to stick out her tongue at him.

The doctor affirmed Brand's diagnosis of bronchitis. He prescribed antibiotics and a potent cough syrup and gave her a lecture about neglecting a cold.

'When can I get back to work?' Briana wanted to know, fearful for the answer.

'Not for a week or so. I want you to stay in bed until the fever is gone. Give me a call, say Monday, and let me know how you are.'

Briana felt a sinking feeling of helplessness. A week off work, or almost a week anyway. What would happen now? She stepped back into the waiting room where Brand was reading a magazine. He looked up, eyebrows raised in question.

'Bronchitis,' she said shortly, waving her prescription at him. 'I have to go to a pharmacy for some medicine.' If he said 'I told you so' she wasn't responsible for her reaction. She looked at him grimly, waiting, but he did not utter the expected words.

'I'll take you home first and then get it filled for you.'

'What about the shop? Don't you have to go to work?'

'The shop can survive without me for a couple of hours.' He reached for her coat on the rack and held it out to her.

'What about my work room? Who's there?'

'Mrs Stamford. I called her last night.' He opened the door and they left the warmth of the doctor's waiting room for the cold outside.

She coughed and swallowed. 'Can she stay through next week?'

'I haven't asked her yet. Did Fielding say you can't go back to work for a week?'

She nodded miserably, shivering in the cold air. 'I'm sorry.'

He made no comment and they drove back home in a silence punctuated by her coughing.

He left again as soon as she was inside, returning forty minutes later with her medicine. She was back in bed, feeling cold and hot at the same time and exhausted from the constant coughing. He made her some toast and tea and saw to it that she ate it. She had no strength to argue with him and she had to admit that it felt good to have someone take care of her, even though Brand could not be called a patient nurse by any stretch of the imagination.

After he had left with the promise to come back at one, she closed her eyes and went back to sleep. She awoke at half-past twelve, feeling hungry and thirsty. The fever seemed to have subsided a little and the rest had done her good. She stayed in bed, listening for Brand's car, which came a few minutes after one.

She got up on shaky legs, put on her robe and brushed her hair before opening the door.

'How are you feeling?'

'A little better. I slept for a while. That cough syrup the doctor prescribed seems to work.'

He sat down next to her. 'Briana?' His eyes searched hers. 'I wasn't very patient this morning. I'm sorry.'

The look in his eyes made her grow warm. 'It's all right.'

His hand reached out and trailed through her hair. 'I love you, you know.'

She nodded. 'I love you too,' she whispered.

For a while they just sat there, looking at each other.

'Feel like something to eat?' he asked at last. 'Soup?'

She nodded. 'There's a can of chicken noodle.'

'I'll get it.' He got up, tossing the afghan across her legs. 'Keep warm.'

They were eating the soup when they heard a knock on the back door, then almost immediately it opened and Ross called her name from the kitchen. Her heart gave a nervous little leap. Oh, no, not Ross! He entered the room a moment later, carrying a package wrapped in pink-and-silver striped paper with a big silver bow on top.

CHAPTER TEN

SHE watched the men stare at each other warily. The instant hostility that sprang up between them was palpable and the air seemed to crackle with tension.

Briana cleared her throat, then introduced them with a voice that sounded strange in her own ears. They shook hands politely. Then Ross turned to her, handing her the package. His face looked strained.

'How are you doing? I looked in on you earlier and you were sound asleep.'

How could he have come in? she wondered.

'I took the key to the back door last night,' he supplied, as if reading her thoughts. 'I left a note on the door. Are you feeling better?'

She shook her head. 'Not much. I went to the doctor this morning. I have bronchitis.' As if to prove this, she began to cough again.

'I brought you some more orange juice,' Ross said after she'd more or less regained her composure, 'it's in the kitchen. I think I'll go now. I'll leave the key in the door. Let me know if you need anything else.' And without another look at Brand, he turned and stalked out of the room. She heard the back door open and close and then he was gone. She stared at the package in her lap, feeling Brand's eyes on her.

'That was him, wasn't it? The good friend?' There was an odd note to Brand's voice and she looked up at him. His face looked tight.

'What's the matter? Why are you looking at me like that?'

He shoved his hands in his pockets. 'That was him, wasn't it?' he repeated, his voice taut with strain.

'Yes.'

'The man's in love with you, Briana!'

'He has never said that.'

'Oh, for God's sake! You're not blind are you?'

A quiver of anger ran down her back. 'Don't talk to me like that!'

The grey eyes flashed. 'What am I supposed to do?' he demanded in a low, angry voice. 'Say, oh, how nice you have such a good friend? Accept without thought that he was here with you last night? Accept that he has the key to the door, that he comes in here while you're asleep . . .'

'Oh, for heaven's sake don't be such a puritan! I didn't give him the key—he took it. He was worried about me. And I refuse to defend him or myself. There's nothing to apologise for!'

'Briana, I love you. I don't like someone else hanging around you like that.'

She clutched the package in her lap, trying to stay calm. 'You'd better get used to it. He's my friend.'

'Don't be so damned naive, Briana! He's in love with you!'

'Well, there's nothing I can do about it!' She sounded defensive and she knew it. 'I'm not in love with him and he knows it. I've told him so. And it's . . . it's . . . none . . .' she wheezed, 'none . . . of your . . . business.' She began to cough again. She clutched at her chest, tears rolling down her cheeks. The package slid off her lap and landed on the floor with a soft thud. The coughing over, she curled up and lay down on the couch, tears still running hot. 'And you don't own me! Don't tell me what to do with my friends or my life or anything!' She clutched the cushion hard with both hands.

He was kneeling by the couch, his hand stroking her hair, her back. 'I'm sorry,' he said thickly. 'I suppose I'm jealous, or maybe not jealous exactly. I don't know.'

She took a deep breath, finally calming down. It seemed incredible that a man like Brand would confess to these emotions, to make himself so vulnerable. She felt her anger melting away.

'There's no reason to feel that way, Brand. You should know that.' Slowly she sat up, taking a tissue from the box and wiping her eyes and blowing her nose.

He sat down next to her, putting his arm around her and drawing her head on his shoulder. 'I'm sorry I started this. You feel miserable enough already and I made it worse.'

'It's all right.'

He bent down and retrieved the package. 'Why don't you open it?'

Slowly she began to take the paper off, finding a set of pastel-striped cotton flannel sheets. She didn't know whether to laugh or cry. Flannel sheets in pink and silver gift wrap with a bow on top. Oh, Ross, she thought, you're crazy! And then fresh tears welled up in her eyes. The pale coloured stripes blurred into wavering lines and she groped for the box of tissues next to her on the couch. She felt such a pain of regret and sorrow that for a moment all she saw in her mind was Ross, walking home in the icy wind, his jacket open and his blond hair flying.

Brand ran his fingers through her hair, playing with the curls. 'What are you crying about?'

She shook her head. 'I don't even know. I just feel so rotten.'

He studied the sheets on her lap. 'Flannel sheets. Such a romantic present,' he said lightly. 'He can't be too serious about seducing you.' There was humour in his voice, and she gave him a watery smile.

'I was so cold yesterday. I said I needed some to make the bed feel warmer. I didn't mean for him to go out and buy them for me.' She sighed. 'You'd better get away from me. I don't want you to get sick too.'

He put his face in her hair. 'I'll take that risk.'

It felt good to be so close. She wished she could

crawl into his breast pocket and stay there for the rest of the day, just listening to the solid thudding of his heart. The image was soothing and she let out another sigh.

'You didn't eat your soup,' he said after a while. 'I'll warm it up for you. And then I'd better get back to the shop before everything comes screeching to a halt.'

The weekend was a miserable one. Brand kept her company part of the time, making sure she ate and drank enough. Illness did not agree with her and she felt depressed and irritable which in turn made her feel guilty. Ross did not show himself. It bothered her and she wondered what to do.

On Monday she felt considerably better. She called Dr Fielding and asked if she couldn't possibly go back to work the next day, but he was adamant that she should take it easy for a few more days. After that she called Mrs Stamford to find out how everything was going and to see if she needed any help or information over the phone.

Mrs Stamford sounded worried. 'The problem is, Briana, that I don't know if I can come tomorrow or the next few days. Didn't Brand tell you?'

Briana felt her heart sink into her shoes. 'No. Oh, my, I hope he has another solution.'

'It's my other daughter, you see.' Mrs Stamford sounded almost apologetic. 'She's expecting a baby any day now and she has two other little ones and I promised to take care of them. I was supposed to go over there Saturday, but when Brand called I thought I'd better help out here first.'

'Of course. She'll need you, and I'm sure Brand will find a solution.' She sounded considerably more confident than she felt, and by the time she hung up the phone she was truly depressed. Well, maybe the baby would co-operate and not make its entrance into the world for a few more days.

Brand called late in the afternoon. 'I've got a meeting,' he said in his abrupt office voice. 'I don't know what time I'll be able to come by.'

'Don't worry about it, I'm doing fine. I'll promise to have something decent to eat. I'll see you another time.'

'Yes, well, maybe that would be best. I'll probably have to take this guy out to dinner. He's from the Department of Rehabilitation. I'd just as soon send him on his merry way, but I'd better play it cool.' He sounded tired and irritable.

'Did you have a hard day?' she asked carefully.

'We had a few problems in the woodshop, yes, but it's all under control now. I'm glad you're feeling better. I'll call you tomorrow.'

For all the concern in his voice she could have been a mere secretary. Well, she was only a mere supervisor and she was causing him considerable problems by being ill. She should understand this. In the shop he was the big boss with a tremendous responsibility. In his personal life he was a different man, a different personality. Somehow she'd have to learn to deal with this two-sidedness of him, these two so very different expressions of his personality. She really did not know if she was able to. Intellectually she could understand it, emotionally she was having a hard time accepting it.

Her patience was being tested severely three days later. As she had done the last few days, she called the shop to see if Mrs Stamford was still on the job or if the birth of an innocent baby was creating an emergency situation.

'Mrs Stamford isn't here,' said Kathleen. 'Her daughter had a baby last night. Brand is in your work room holding the fort. You want to talk to him?'

Briana felt her heart sink. No, she didn't want to talk to Brand. As a matter of fact, it was the last thing she wanted. She sighed. 'I think I'd better.'

'Just a moment, I'll put you through. By the way, how are you? Brand said you have bronchitis.'

'I do. It's getting better, though, but the doctor won't let me out of the house yet.'

'Well, you'd better get better fast. We need you. Let me find Brand for you.'

'Yes?' came the short reply a moment later.

'Is there anything I can do from this end?' she asked.

'You can tell me which way those coupons need to be collated, and do we seal the envelopes? And Jill's about finished with her work, and what else is there for her to do?'

She told him about the coupons. 'And Jill can do more bath sheets. There's another roll of fabric in the store room, somebody needs to cut them at the right length though.'

'Which is what?'

'I don't remember. It's in the file. Second drawer of the big filing cabinet.'

'Who does the cutting?'

'I do.'

He swore under his breath. 'Anyone else who can do that?'

'Sally can probably do it. You'll have to show her and watch her carefully.'

There were more questions. She tried to answer them as best she could, but the details were legion, things she didn't even think about any more, things he had no idea about and that would cause problems if he didn't deal with them correctly. Dispiritedly, she stared out the window. It was a depressing sight. Rain poured down from a leaden sky and a stormy wind lashed the bare trees unmercifully. Dead leaves swept across the road and swirled through the turbulent air. The world looked grey. She felt grey herself. She wished she weren't alone in this little old house, alone with an old woman's memories. Would the house ever

really be hers? Would it ever feel like home? She
sighed. The idleness was getting to her now that she
was feeling a little better. Being used to being so busy
every day, it was suddenly hard to take.

Half an hour later Brand was back on the phone, his
voice tight with restrained fury. Obviously, things
were not going well. Brand was not familiar enough
with the work being done in the workroom. He didn't
know the people well enough. It was an impossible
situation! She'd never felt so helpless in her life. And
it seemed so unnecessary. She was feeling fine, well-
rested, and getting bored hanging around the house
doing nothing. There was no reason why she couldn't
get back to work if she took it easy.

'Listen, why don't I just come over for an hour or
so, just to get the work sorted out?'

'You stay right where you are,' he said irritably. 'I'll
manage. Fielding said a week, and that's exactly what
you'll do!'

'But I'm feeling all right!'

'That's what you said last week! If you had been
smart enough to take a couple of days then to get
over that cold, you wouldn't have come down with
bronchitis!'

Her hand gripped the receiver and her knuckles
were white. 'Don't shout at me!'

'You need shouting at! You acted irresponsibly and
see where it got us!'

Irresponsible! She was shaking with fury. 'God, I
hate you,' she said in a low voice, slamming the phone
down. She curled up on the couch, wrapping the
afghan around her, feeling tears welling up in her eyes.
I can't stand him, she thought. Oh, God, I can't stand
him when he's like that!

The phone rang an hour later. She let it ring. It
went on and on and it jangled her nerves, but she
didn't move from the couch. She'd turned on the TV
earlier and she watched it with fanatical concentration

trying to block out the ringing. Eventually it stopped. Half an hour later it began again. Once more she let it ring. Let him figure things out for himself, she thought bitterly. She didn't have to submit herself to his shouting. *Irresponsible*, he'd said. It hurt more than she was willing to admit, but the word kept echoing in her mind.

She heard knocking at the back door and her heart leaped. Ross! She jumped off the couch and rushed to the kitchen. Through the window she saw him standing outside, hair dripping, coat collar pulled up against the wind. Quickly she turned the key, opened the door and let him in.

'You're home,' he said, which seemed a strange sort of greeting.

'Of course I'm home. Take off your coat. I'll get you a towel.'

He draped his coat over the back of a kitchen chair and rubbed his hair and face with the towel Briana gave him. 'Is your phone working? I called you twice this morning and you didn't answer. I'd seen your car outside, so I wondered what the hell was going on.' He put the towel down, his hair sticking up in wet peaks all over his head.

'Oh,' she said, 'it was you. The phone calls, I mean.'

He frowned. 'Who did you think it was? Why didn't you answer?'

'I would have if I'd known it was you. I'm sorry.' She paused. 'I'm glad you came. I haven't seen you for days.'

'I kept seeing that old Pontiac in front of your house. I figured you were well taken care of.' His tone was carefully bland and she looked at his face searchingly.

'I can always use friends, you know.'

She saw his jaw harden and anger suddenly leaped in his eyes. 'Dammit, Briana, I don't want to be your friend!'

'I'm sorry,' she said miserably, hugging herself and shivering for some unknown reason. It wasn't cold in the house.

He advanced towards her, putting his hands on her upper arms and looking into her eyes. 'I came here for two reasons,' he said tightly. 'Firstly, because I was worried about you when you didn't answer the damned phone, and secondly I want to know where I stand.'

She stepped away from him. 'Ross, nothing has changed!' She spread her hands in a helpless gesture. 'I told you, I want to be friends, nothing more.'

'Briana, I don't know what idiotic notion you have about us being *friends*, but it's just not going to work, at least not from my side. I've tried to be patient, but . . .' He shrugged, defeated.

Briana was silent. There was nothing to say.

'What about this character that was here, your boss, Edwards? Is he having more success than I am?'

'Oh, for God's sake, Ross, don't start that!'

He came closer again, looking at her darkly. 'He was here off and on all weekend, dispensing, no doubt, a lot of tender loving care. What am I supposed to think?'

'Whatever you like!'

'My God, Briana, I don't understand you! You don't even like the guy. You couldn't even stand him, you said.'

'You're right,' she said bitterly, 'I can't. That's why I wasn't answering the telephone. I thought it was him—he,' she corrected herself.

'Fighting already?' The sarcasm was hard to miss. She didn't know easy-going Ross could be so hard and bitter.

'We've been fighting from day one. It's nothing new.'

'So what the hell do you want with that guy?'

'Ross, I don't need to answer that! I don't want to fight with you. Please, be reasonable!'

'Reasonable! What is it that I've been for the last few months?' He paused, his face oddly white. 'Briana, don't you understand how I feel about you?'

She nodded, seeing the despair in his eyes, feeling wretched. 'I'm sorry, Ross. I'm more sorry than you'll ever know.'

He stared at her in silence. 'So am I,' he said at last. His voice was toneless and the bleakness in his eyes tore at her heart. He took his wet coat from the chair and pulled it on. 'Goodbye, Briana.'

Her throat closed and not a word would come. Her eyes misted over as she watched him walk out the door. Briefly she saw his shape move past the window, then he was gone.

Just after six that evening Brand's car drew up in front of the house. She let him in without a word.

He gave her a searching look. 'How are you doing?'

'Just fine, thank you,' she said coldly. She plopped herself back into her chair, picking up the bowl of stew she'd been eating, ignoring him.

'What's the matter?' he asked, still standing in the middle of the room, coat on.

'You. And don't pretend you don't understand.' She spooned stew into her mouth. Her hand was shaking.

He sighed. 'I'm sorry I lost my temper this morning, but I wasn't exactly having the time of my life.'

'Neither was I! And to be perfectly honest with you, I can't stand your overbearing, short-tempered big-boss attitude! I don't know what comes over you when you enter that shop!' She fished a piece of carrot out of her bowl and chewed it.

'You said you hated me,' he said tonelessly.

She closed her eyes briefly. 'I did. For a moment I really did.'

'Not any more?'

She shook her head numbly, not looking at him. She loved him, oh God, she did love him, but how was she ever going to get used to that unbearable side of his character?

'You have to understand,' he said, 'that it's the only way I could make that place run. Somebody has to be boss. Somebody has to keep on top of things.'

'Well, you don't have to be so rigid and high-handed about it! And you don't have to accuse me of . . . of . . . irresponsibility!' Her voice shook. 'I didn't get bronchitis on purpose! I've had a number of colds in my life and they've always just gone away.' She clenched the spoon, taking an unsteady breath. 'And for you to call me *irresponsible* when I've worked like a mule, when I've put myself into this job . . .' Her voice trailed away and she bit her lip hard to keep from bursting into tears.

'Briana, I'm sorry.' He shrugged out of his coat and tossed it on to the couch. 'Come here.' He took the bowl and spoon out of her hands and drew her up into his arms. 'I've always known how hard you work. I know it even better now that I've tried to take over for you. I'm not taking you for granted. Please, don't ever think that. I'm sorry I hurt you. I shouldn't have said that.'

She didn't reply, still too hurt to forgive him so easily. Stiffly she leaned again him, unable to yield to him.

'Please don't do that to me,' he whispered in her ear. 'Don't stand there as if you don't want me to hold you.'

'I'm sorry!' she cried, straining against his hold. 'But I can't switch on and off like you do! I know I should be graceful and accept your apology, but . . . but the fact is that I don't feel very forgiving right now. I'm angry, Brand! I'm angry and I'm hurt and the best thing you can do is to leave me alone.'

His arms fell away from her body. He took a step

back. 'All right,' he said coolly as he walked to the door. 'I will.'

But the cool tone of his voice belied the expression in his eyes. She knew she had hurt him, and it didn't feel good.

She went back to work the next day. Everyone was happy to see her again. They were all eager to get back to the normal day-to-day routine. Irregularities upset the balance and confused them. Brand avoided her workroom and she didn't see him at all. She tried not to think about him, she felt tense all day.

It was just after the workers had left and she was cleaning up, that Kathleen called her from the front desk.

'There's somebody from the fire department here who wants to speak to you,' she said.

'The *fire department*?'

'Yes. Shall I send him in?'

'No, no . . . I'll be right there.'

The fire department? she wondered as she quickly walked to the front office. A greying man in suit and tie awaited her.

'Are you Mrs Briana Crossley?'

'Yes.'

'Are you the owner of the property on Williams Road, number 103?'

She nodded, feeling a sudden horrible premonition.

'We had a call earlier this afternoon. I'm afraid there was a fire.'

'Oh, no!' she moaned. 'Not my house.' How could that be? A thousand questions ran through her mind. She'd turned everything off that morning. She was so careful always to check everything. 'It can't be!' she whispered. 'Are you sure?'

He nodded. 'Quite sure, ma'am.'

'How bad is it? I've got to go there . . . I . . .'

'I'm sorry, but there isn't much left. It went up like

a torch. The men did what they could, but they were too late. A neighbour reported it when it was already burning considerably.'

'But how? What caused it?' She sank weakly into a chair.

'Probably the wiring. It was an old house. Electrical fires are not uncommon.' He gave her a sympathetic look. 'Just be grateful it didn't happen at night while you were asleep.'

She stared unseeingly at the carpeting, not taking in the other things he said, noticing only vaguely that he finally left. When Kathleen put a cup of coffee down on the table next to her, she came to her feet. 'Thanks, Kathleen, but I've got to go. I've got to see ... Where's my purse?' She raked her fingers through her hair. *It can't be true!* she kept thinking. *It can't be true! There must have been a mistake ...*

The door to Brand's office opened and for a moment they stared at each other.

'What's going on?' he said at last.

'Briana's house burned down,' explained Kathleen. 'Somebody from the fire department was just here.'

'I've got to go,' Briana repeated. 'My purse ... it must be in my office.'

'I'll get it.' Kathleen rushed out, coming back a moment later with Briana's coat as well as her purse.

'Thanks.' She put her arms in the sleeves and pulled it on.

'Come with me.' Brand took her elbow and without another word steered her through the door and out to his car. He opened the door and helped her inside. She stared blindly out the window.

'I can't believe it,' she whispered. 'Everything gone.'

'Is that what they said?'

She nodded. 'You know,' she said dully, 'I don't think I was meant to live in that house.'

He gave her a quick sideways glance. 'What do you mean?'

She shrugged. 'It never felt quite like it really was my house. I couldn't get away from the idea that it was still my grandmother's.' She smiled thinly. 'I had a terrible time cleaning it out, getting rid of things. I didn't feel I had the right, somehow. They weren't my things. I didn't know what I should do with them.' She sighed. 'I guess I won't have that problem any more.'

They took the last bend in the road and then it was there for them to see. She got out of the car, her heart aching at the scene of devastation. Nothing but burned wood and twisted metal was left of what once had been a house. Furniture, appliances—everything black and wet and unrecognisable.

She stared at the scorched ruins, feeling sick with pain and sorrow. All gone—Grandma's house, the lacy curtains, pictures, the china cats. All the memories— gone. Tears were rolling silently down her cheeks. 'I'm sorry, Grandma,' she whispered.

She turned away abruptly and walked back to the car. She didn't want to look at it any more. She never wanted to see it again.

Brand slid behind the steering wheel, turning towards her and drawing her to him. She took a deep breath, willing the tears to stop. His arms felt good around her. He stroked her head.

'I'm sorry, Briana,' he said quietly.

'It was just an old house,' she said in an effort to see things in perspective.

'But it meant a lot to you.'

'Yes.'

'Was there anything of value there?'

She thought of the old furniture, the ancient refrigerator, the plaques on the wall. 'Everything.' She smiled thinly. 'Besides that, nothing.'

'What about your personal belongings?'

She hadn't thought about that. Leather suitcases, 300-dollar dresses, Italian shoes, jewellery ... She shrugged.

'I don't care about that.'

'We'll stop in town and buy you whatever you need for the next few days.'

'Yes,' she said, half-dazed by the realisation that she had nothing left except the clothes she had on and the contents of her purse.

He took her home and fixed dinner for them both—a steak, salad and crusty french bread. It looked good, but she wasn't hungry.

'I'll need to find another place to live,' she said tonelessly, overwhelmed by the idea of starting all over. Maybe she could rent an apartment, or a town house.

'You don't need another place, Briana. You belong here, with me.' He reached across the table and took her hand. 'I want us to get married. I want you to live with me in this house, make a real home out of it.'

'Oh, Brand,' she said softly, 'aren't you going a little too fast?'

'Why? What reason is there to wait? I don't want a long-drawn-out affair with you. I've made up my mind. I know what I want.'

She looked down at her half-eaten steak. 'Just yesterday we were shouting at each other. We obviously haven't worked out our relationship very well.'

His eyes looked at her intently. 'Briana, there'll be adjustments to make, I don't deny that. In any relationship there are *always* adjustments. I certainly don't want a stagnant relationship. If we wait until we have it all figured out we'll be waiting till Doomsday.'

He pushed his plate away and came to his feet. He drew her out of her chair and put his arms around her.

'I love you,' he said. 'I want to be with you. I need

you, Briana. Please, marry me.' There was a deep urgency in his voice and he held her close against him.

She could think of a number of reasons why she shouldn't, but none of them stacked up against the powerful emotion of love. And if she loved him, she would have to trust him. That's what it all came down to. Trust, no guarantees.

She closed her eyes. She was trembling and her heart hammered with fear. 'All right,' she whispered, 'I'll marry you.'

He let out a deep sigh. 'We'll be happy, I promise we'll be happy.' His lips trailed over her temple, her closed eyes, her cheek. His hand wandered restlessly over her back and she sensed his desire in the urgency of his touch.

'How are you feeling now?' he whispered.

'I'm all right.'

'All right enough?'

She nodded.

'I want you,' he said huskily, his lips finding hers in sudden feverish passion. She felt his arousal when she returned his kiss with a need of her own. She wanted him too. She loved him, this infuriating man, and her love was greater than any of the anger and the hurt he caused her. He wasn't an easy man, he wasn't perfect, but he certainly was a man worth loving. He was a man with strong passions, a man who fought for what he believed in, who didn't give up when the going got tough.

Her legs were rather unsteady as they moved to the bedroom, his arm tightly around her as if he were afraid she'd run off. He put her down on the bed, slipping her sweater over her head and unfastening her bra. He put his face down on her breast, lying still for a few endless moments, just holding her. She put her hands on his head, stroking his hair, love and rapture rising like a warm tide. She felt the pounding of his heart and her body ached for him. Slowly his hand reached down and unzipped her jeans and he kissed her belly. She felt lighter and lighter, feeling no weight at all, not even the bed beneath her, floating through warm seas of sensual delight.

He was with her in bed, his clothes hastily discarded. And it was the most wonderful feeling to have him so close, to feel the warmth of his skin against her own. She pulled his head towards her, kissing him on the mouth, her hands stroking him, loving him. For a long time they pleased each other, longer than she'd ever thought possible, reaching heights of delight she'd never known. Afterwards, she clung to him, feeling such a depth of emotion, of love and tenderness, of gratitude and relief that tears came to her eyes.

He kissed her face. 'You're crying,' he said incredulously. 'Briana, why?'

She shook her head, smiling through her tears. 'I'm happy. I'm just happy.'

He laughed softly, hugging her. 'You're a very strange, lady, and I love you.'

'I love you too.'

'Will you still love me on Monday when we're back at work?'

'I'll try. I've never loved a tyrant before. I don't know how good I'll be at that.'

'And I'll try to be a little more human on the job.' He played with her curls. 'I know I can be difficult, but I do love you and I do want to make you happy. Do you believe me?'

She nodded. She felt light with joy and relief, the fear gone. *Everything will be all right*, she said to herself. *I'm safe with him.*

He smiled down at her, his heart in his eyes. 'Welcome home, my love.'

Harlequin Presents

Coming Next Month

Available in February wherever paperback books are sold, or through Harlequin Reader Service:

In the U.S.
P.O. Box 1397
Buffalo, N.Y.
14240-1397

In Canada
P.O. Box 603
Fort Erie, Ontario
L2A 5X3

Six exciting series for you every month... from Harlequin

Harlequin Romance·
The series that started it all

Tender, captivating and heartwarming...
love stories that sweep you off to faraway places
and delight you with the magic of love.

♦

Harlequin Presents·
Powerful contemporary love stories...as individual as the women who read them

The No. 1 romance series...
exciting love stories for you, the woman of today...
a rare blend of passion and dramatic realism.

♦

Harlequin Superromance®
It's more than romance... it's Harlequin Superromance

A sophisticated, contemporary romance-fiction
series, providing you with a longer,
more involving read...a richer mix of complex plots,
realism and adventure.

HARLEQUIN HISTORICAL

Explore love with Harlequin in the Middle Ages, the Renaissance, in the Regency, the Victorian and other eras.

Relive within these books the endless ages of romance, set against authentic historical backgrounds. Two new historical love stories published each month.

ATTRACTIVE, SPACE SAVING BOOK RACK

Display your most prized novels on this handsome and sturdy book rack. The hand-rubbed walnut finish will blend into your library decor with quiet elegance, providing a practical organizer for your favorite hard-or soft-covered books.

Only $9.95

Approximately 16" x 8" when assembled

Assembles in seconds!

To order, rush your name, address and zip code, along with a check or money order for $10.70 ($9.95 plus 75¢ postage and handling) (New York residents add appropriate sales tax), payable to *Harlequin Reader Service* to:

In the U.S.

Harlequin Reader Service
Book Rack Offer
901 Fuhrmann Blvd.
P.O. Box 1325
Buffalo, NY 14269-1325

Offer not available in Canada.

BKR-1